# Hangman's Lot

Amidst an Apache uprising Marshal Dan Mannion is riding back from Mexico with the notorious killer Nathan Trump as his prisoner and with Trump's murderous kin dogging his tail. Then into this mix comes Sister Lucy, a nun.

Or is she?

Now there is even more confusion with many unanswered questions. Why, for example is Nathan's father, Zachariah Trump, so anxious to avoid clashing with the friendly Indians with whom he trades? And why is Hunting Wolf, the leader of the Indians, so keen to meet up with Zachariah Trump?

Meanwhile, back in Tuteville, a rejected competitor for the hand of Rosie O'Sullivan, whom Dan intends to marry when he returns, plots to have Mannion removed from the scene should he make it back. There sure is trouble awaiting the lawman!

# Hangman's Lot

## BEN COADY

**A Black Horse Western**

ROBERT HALE · LONDON

ISBN 0 7090 7155 8

Robert Hale Limited
Clerkenwell House
Clerkenwell Green
London EC1R 0HT

Typeset by
Derek Doyle & Associates, Liverpool.
Printed and bound in Great Britain by
Antony Rowe Limited, Wiltshire

# ONE

Dan Mannion looked out across the desert at the smoke puffing from the hills, and reckoned that he'd need the devil's own luck to keep his scalp. He had a lot of country to cross, and more dangers to face than he'd care for, before he'd make it back to Tuteville.

If he made it back to Tuteville.

In the last couple of days, Mannion had travelled through a spate of burned-out wagons, charred homesteads, and rotting corpses. Holding on to his scalp would not be easy. Indians weren't the only risk to Mannion's survival. There was Nathan Trump, the handcuffed man supping coffee a few feet away from him, and his kin. Trump was an evil-minded, murderous son-of-a-bitch, who would take even greater pleasure than any Apache would in slitting Dan Mannion's throat.

Back in Tuteville, Trump was facing a hangman's noose for murder. Mannion had tracked him to a Mex village, where Trump visited a whore who liked his violent streak when bedding a woman. It was a streak common to the Trump quartet, and they had as few qualms about rape as they had about robbery and murder.

In fact, as Mannion had listened outside the whore's bedroom door before shackling Nathan Trump, the outlaw was relaying to her the sordid details of his pleasure with an Apache woman whom he'd violated, and had then shared with his brothers and pa for a couple of weeks until, despairing, the woman had thrown herself off the top of a canyon.

Nathan Trump had boasted, 'I tell ya, Conchita honey, that 'Pache, Wild Flower, Pa said her name was, him knowin' 'Pache lingo, gave me and my kin wild nights.' He laughed. 'Pa, the horny old bastard, took her more times than any of us.'

Mannion had no doubt that word of Nathan Trump's being taken prisoner had quickly reached Nathan's pa, Zachariah, and his brothers Frank and Jed. The murderous quartet were never far apart.

'Scared, Marshal?' Trump taunted Dan Mannion. The outlaw's snide smirk raised the lawman's hackles. Trump held out his hands. 'Take these cuffs off, let me ride. You'll travel a lot faster, safer, too. I'll tell Pa you let me go. He'll tell the 'Paches to let you ride free of trouble.'

'Get on your horse,' Mannion ordered sourly. 'And shut your damn mouth!'

Nathan Trump strolled casually to his horse. Dan Mannion knew that the outlaw's relaxed mood was justified. The Trumps were safe from Apache anger. Zachariah Trump had traded enough guns and rotgut with them to ensure that. Trump's offer had tempted him, and maybe he'd have yielded to that temptation, if he thought for one second that the outlaw would keep his word. Mannion vaulted into the saddle, bone-weary. He had been on the trail for more than a week, sleeping with one eye open.

'You ain't goin' to make it, lawman,' Trump sniggered.

'Don't push me, Trump,' the marshal growled. 'Plenty of soft sand around here to plant you in.'

'You're in real trouble, Mannion,' Trump taunted.

Dan Mannion thought: Tell me something I don't know.

He had, during the torturous days since he'd set out in pursuit of Nathan Trump, become painfully aware of the advantages the Trump brood held over him. They knew the terrain like their own back yard, having spent long spells hiding out in the desert. They had grown used to the harsh climate and counted the Apache as their friends, along with a host of other black-hearted knaves with whom they had shared the desert roosts while on the run from the law.

Dan Mannion had not been in the desert for a long time. He had spent the last ten years putting on lard as the Tuteville marshal, whose only trouble might be a saloon bust-up on a Saturday night, and even that was a rare event. But in one vicious minute, Nathan Trump had changed the town's quiet nature, when he had killed a man for simply bumping into him, and had then dispatched Mannion's deputy, the old-timer Saul Harrington, when he tried to arrest him.

Mannion had been out of town following the trail of rustlers raiding up from Mexico, and had returned to meet two funerals on Main.

Dan Mannion was not a desert-smart man, the Trumps were. The gang knew the desert, its canyons, draws, ravines, and most important, its waterholes. They also knew what could and could not be eaten.

Up to now, he had not seen sign of the Apaches, except their smoke. That's what really worried him. Indians had a way of biding their time, lulling a man into a sense of false security, which they then took an evil glee in shattering.

As he reacted jitterly to a clatter of shale rattling down from high up in the canyon, Nathan

Trump's mocking chuckle did nothing to sweeten Dan Mannion's mood.

'Might be a 'Pache up there, Marshal' he sneered. 'Might be my pa, too. Like the 'Pache, Pa's invisible 'til he slits your damn throat. Can sneak up on a man like a ghost!'

Mannion's grey eyes scanned the canyon's high reaches. Nothing. His nerves jangled as the dislodged shale gathered more on its way down and echoed discordantly through the canyon.

Mannion made tracks towards the canyon's westerly exit. He was reckoning on about another day before he reached the old prospectors' trail he was aiming for. He wasn't sure if the trail still existed. It had been years since he'd heard of anyone using it as a means to reach Tuteville. It was a constantly changing country, moulded and remoulded on a continual basis by the harsh climate. Trails and tracks changed, sometimes out of recognition, and other times completely vanished. Mannion could only pray that Rourke's Trail still existed. If it didn't, he'd have to backtrack, and the country to his rear was clouded by the smoke of Apache raiding-parties. If he had to retrace his trail, he'd lose precious time, and would also risk running smack into the Trumps. Dan Mannion had little doubt that Zachariah Trump and Nathan's two brothers Frank and Jed were on his tail.

Apaches or Trumps, it didn't make much difference. Either would kill him.

The cover of the canyon slipped behind the Tuteville marshal. He eyed the flat, open desert with trepidation. It was terrain where a man would have no hiding place from watching eyes. There were other trails, safer trails, which he could take, but they were longer by at least two days, and with Indians and the Trumps snapping at his heels, time was running out. He'd called on his luck a couple of times already, and he hoped that there was still enough in his account to see him safely to Rourke's Trail. If he reached the old prospectors' trail, he figured that he'd make it back in one piece to Tuteville. Besides delivering Nathan Trump to the gallows, there was one other mighty important reason why he wanted to make it back.

Her name was Rosie O'Sullivan.

An hour later, Dan Mannion had to call on his luck once again. Lying flat in a shallow dip in the ground while a party of Apaches rode past, he held his Colt .45 on Nathan Trump.

'Whisper and you're dead,' he promised the outlaw.

It was common knowledge that the Trump gang were friendly with the Apache, and Mannion had seen in Nathan's Trump's hard eyes the temptation to call out to them. The bucks passed so close to Mannion, he gagged at the foul smell of the animal fat on their glistening bodies. If an Indian glanced to his right, he couldn't miss seeing them. Luckily the marshal had heard their chatter and had time to seek cover, meagre as it was.

Draped around the bucks' necks were the scalps of their latest victims. The fetid stench of the clotted blood on the hair nauseated Mannion. Most of the scalps were female, and the marshal had no doubt, judging by the bucks' lewd and lurid gestures, that the women whose scalps they had taken had suffered long and hard. Dan Mannion's blood sizzled in his veins with anger.

Though Mannion's warning struck a sobering note with the outlaw, risking the marshal's gun was not the deciding factor in the outlaw's decision not to hail the Indians. His fear was that they would set upon him before he had a chance to explain who he was. Although his pa and his brothers had often traded with the Indians, he had seldom joined them in their parleying, quoting dislike of the Apache as the reason, when in fact the real reason was that he dreaded being anywhere near them. There was a long trail to Tuteville. Opportunities would present themselves. And by now his kin must be scouring the trails to rescue him. However, as the gap between

11

them and the Indians widened, temptation to risk hailing the war party crept back.

'Blink and you'll meet the devil, Trump!' the Tuteville marshal warned.

# TWO

Zachariah Trump, for the cut-throat bastard he was, was a deceptively friendly looking man. His chest-length, snow-white beard, scraggy at the ends due to his long sojourn in the desert and Mexico, hiding out from the lawmen of at least three territories, gave him the appearance of an Old Testament prophet. His saintly visage was what made him such a successful villian. It would be difficult to believe that behind such a benign dial, beat a heart poisoned and owned by Satan.

Annoyed by the sight of the deserted, twilit country ahead, Zachariah went back down the ridge to join his sons in the ravine they'd chosen for the night.

'Well, Pa,' Jed Trump, a rake-thin man with Apache features enquired, 'any sign?'

Zachariah Trump had not been particular about his women, seeing no need to have all his sons out of one womb. Jed was the issue of an

Apache squaw. Frank Trump, the eldest, sported the red hair of an Irish saloon dove. Nathan, his youngest and most prized, he being the most like him, was the issue of a dalliance with a preacher's wife, who had tired of being bedded in accordance with the Good Book.

'Nothin',' Zachariah growled sourly.

Frank Trump griped, 'So how long more're we goin' to ride our asses raw, Pa?'

Zachariah's eyes hooded dangerously. 'For as long as it damn well takes. That's how long.' Trump senior landed his fist squarely on his eldest son's jaw, sending him sprawling back from the fire he was setting to cook the evening meal. Of his three sons, Zachariah liked Frank least, had done ever since he was fifteen years old and had hesitated in killing a lawman, whom Zachariah had offered to his son, trussed like a chicken.

'That boy's got a yella streak that worries me,' he'd commented to a sidekick of the time.

Zachariah had then shot the lawman through the head, and made Frank sleep that night tied to the dead man. Even the murdering hardcases whom Zachariah Trump associated with had blanched at what he'd done to his own boy.

Frank Trump stifled the overwhelming temptation to go for his gun. Hatred of his father was a long-festering sore, which the old buzzard insisted on opening time and time again. Zachariah could read Frank Trump's every thought. There were times, like right now, when he wished that Frank would show the kind of devil's spit which Jed and Nathan had. The way Zachariah figured, if Frank went for his gun, it would solve a problem. If Frank beat him to the draw and killed him, then he'd no longer feel the sense of shame he felt when he looked at his eldest son. And if he killed Frank, the same would apply.

Jed Trump, cold blue eyes glinting, licked cracked, dry lips in anticipation of a bust-up. The world was getting too small a place for his pa and Frank to co-exist. The time could not be far off before one killed the other. Who won was of no interest to Jed Trump. He'd weep no tears for either man.

Courage failing him, much to Zachariah's disgust, Frank said, 'Sure, Pa. We'll keep lookin' for Nathan as long as it takes.'

'Why worry, anyways,' Jed said. 'Way I figure, the 'Pache will most likely have Mannion's scalp by now, and you bein' real cosy with the 'Paches, Pa, they ain't goin' to harm Nathan.' Jed pondered. 'What I don't understand, Pa, is why we ain't goin' hell for leather, 'stead of sneakin' 'round? The 'Paches bein' no threat t'us.'

Zachariah Trump had a secret which explained his caution. The leader of the renegades, Hunting Wolf, was a blood thirsty redskin he'd unloaded a shipment of useless rifles on, several of which had exploded in his bucks' faces. Apaches had long, unforgiving memories, and Hunting Wolf's was longer and more unforgiving than any other. If Nathan fell into Hunting Wolf's clutches, he'd die the slowest, cruellest death that the Apache could think up. Having seen some of Hunting Wolf's handiwork, an ice-cold finger trickled along Zachariah's spine. There was no way he was going to risk being roasted alive by Hunting Wolf, even for Nathan.

Ten miles south of where Zachariah Trump was doing his pondering, a scout was telling Hunting Wolf about the white-bearded man who had traded the exploding rifles. Hunting Wolf's eyes glowed like hot coals, so intense was his anger.

'Where you see Trump?'

The scout replied, 'The place the white man calls Bony Ridge.'

'Alone?'

'Two men ride with him,' the scout said. 'Sons.'

Hunting Wolf gleefully called an old man to him. 'Build good fires, Running Stream,' he ordered. 'Soon we will roast Trump and his sons over them.'

As the desert moon rode through a star-filled sky, Dan Mannion's thoughts turned to Rosie O'

Sullivan, a blue-eyed, blonde beauty, whom he was planning on proposing to the second he got back to Tuteville. Of course, Rosie might refuse his proposal. His only guide to her feelings for him were her visits to the law office and her little kindnesses, like the broth she often arrived with on cold nights. It seemed to Dan Mannion that a beautiful woman like Rosie, who could have any man, including Luther Barrett, Tuteville's richest man, eating out of her hand, could have put her time to better use, if that's what she wanted. Maybe his brains had been scrambled by her attention to him, but Dan Mannion figured he was reading correctly the purpose and intention of Rosie's visits. At least that was his hope. Though what she saw in a mere badge-toter, with so many shekel-rich men ready to worship at her feet, puzzled and amazed the marshal. He took comfort, and hope, too, from Rosie's plea before he had set out after Nathan Trump, that when he popped the question on his return, her answer would be yes.

'Notify the US marshal, Dan,' she'd pleaded. 'Let him hunt Trump'

Dan had explained. 'Nathan Trump's my problem, Rosie. And I don't hand my problems to any other man to solve.'

Rosie's blue eyes had glowed proudly. 'You're a principled and good man, Dan Mannion,' she'd said, in a voice as warm as winter fire. 'You'll make some lucky woman a fine husband.'

Now, pondering in the desert moonlight, Dan Mannion wondered if that moment hadn't been the right one to pop the question? He had surely thought about it. But what if he had, and had not made it back? A sudden and terrible fear suddenly gripped Dan Mannion at the thought of losing the prize that was, he reckoned, his for the asking.

Of course, there was Luther Barrett to consider. He saw Rosie O'Sullivan through the same tinted spectacles and would not willingly step aside. It worried Dan that his absence would give the owner of the Big B, the territory's biggest ranch, a free hand. Dan Mannion's regret at not having asked Rosie to be his wife before he left town now acted as a knife plunged deep into his heart. Maybe, with him not around, Rosie's head would be turned by Luther Barrett's attentions. He was, after all, a formidable presence. Men doffed their hats at the boss of the Big B, and stepped off the boardwalk to let him pass. Folk kowtowed to Luther Barrett. Dan fretted that with him not around, Rosie might be swayed by being on the arm of such an important man. Mannion was instantly ashamed of his mean-spirited thoughts. Rosie O'Sullivan was an independent-minded woman, who would not be influenced by the trappings that went with Luther Barrett's favour.

Barrett had taken every chance to boast that soon Rosie O'Sullivan would be the mistress of the Big B, a mighty temptation and sumptuous prize for any woman. Certainly, Dan Mannion's thousand dollars in the bank and his marshal's pay came noway near providing the kind of luxury a man of Luther Barrett's resources could provide Rosie with. With Mannion she would not have the hand-to-mouth existence that was the lot of many Western women. A marshal would in many women's eyes be something of a catch. However, as Luther Barrett's wife, Rosie would live like royalty.

Proposing to Rosie O'Sullivan took courage. Like Dan, Barrett had not yet worked up the steam to do so. Her haughty, stand-offish manner, had fazed both men. But Mannion reckoned that Rosie's snootiness was a front, to scare off unsuitable suitors. A woman of Rosie's allure, beauty, and curvy proportions invited pestering. In the West, where women aged and became bitter fast, Rosie was a bloom in a desert. 'Blink and I'll be back,' Dan Mannion had promised her. But Nathan Trump had been hard to run to ground, and with renegade Apaches on the prowl, added to the danger of being overtaken by Nathan Trump's murderous kin, the marshal had had to watch every step he'd taken. His sluggish progress had eaten up time.

Conscious of his promise, and fearful of Luther Barrett's unfettered access to Rosie, Dan had, more than once, thought about cutting Nathan Trump loose and bolting for Tuteville. But if he did that it would be the first dishonest act in his years as a lawman, and as a man. He had come up with a hundred arguments to justify his action, but each one stuck in his craw. He wore an untarnished star, and took pride in that fact, as he was sure Rosie O'Sullivan did, too. If he returned to Tuteville without Trump, he'd have to lie to Rosie, and that would be no way to begin what he hoped would be many long and fruitful years together, if he made it out of the bind he found himself in. All the arguments and reasons sifted through, Dan Mannion was left with only one course of action. That was to do all he could to deliver Nathan Trump to a hangman's rope.

Rosie O'Sullivan tossed restlessly. A storm had come up, and its lonely wind filled her with melancholy. It had been an age, it seemed, since Dan Mannion had ridden off in search of Nathan Trump, and sleep had left with him. Through her bedroom window, Rosie watched the towering trees that surrounded the small house bend under the wind's gusting and wondered where Dan might be, and if he was safe. Dan Mannion hadn't been out of her thoughts. She had hoped, despaired, prayed, and cursed - berated and beseeched God with equal fervour. Why had he let Nathan Trump ride into Tuteville? Then, in brighter and more hope-filled moments, she saw the outlaw's visit as the catalyst that had opened her eyes and made sense of all those trips to the law office for which, at the time, she had come up with a flurry of reasons other than the one that was most obvious, that she was in love with Dan Mannion. Rosie O'Sullivan now knew that, were any misfortune to befall Dan, her life would be over and done with. Of course, in her darker moments, she feared that he might not feel the same way about her, and panicked. However, she had decided, that should Dan Mannion return safely, she'd move heaven and hell to change his mind, if it needed changing.

Rosie O'Sullivan began to pray silently and fervently.

# THREE

Dan Mannion crept cautiously up the rise of ground, testing each step before he took it, though he reckoned that he could have brought a hundred boulders tumbling down without the drunken Apaches noticing. He cast a careful eye on the scene in the ravine below, and his face soured with anger and disgust. A pair of wagons were on their sides. Clothes and scattered wooden cases were strewn around, most of their wine bottles discarded and empty. Those remaining were being guzzled by the drunken Indians. Other braves were enjoying the six women, who lay naked and violated beneath the bucks, with more lining up to use them. One of the women, older than the others, lay with her throat slit, her head hairless, flies swarming on the scalping wound. A buck danced about holding the woman's scalp aloft, the fresh blood from the trophy dripping on to his bronzed body.

Dan had heard tell of a group of French nuns

who had set out from a place thirty miles north of Tuteville, called Darby's Landing, to bring the Christian gospel to the heathen Apache. Looked like they'd not taken kindly to the sisters' efforts to bring them the good news. One of the Indians was prancing about dressed in a nun's habit.

The marshal slid back down the slope to where he had handcuffed Nathan Trump to a tree, gagged. Dan unlocked the handcuffs, stepped back, Colt cocked, while the killer snapped the handcuffs back on his wrists.

'Separate your hands and tug on the cuffs,' Mannion ordered. Nathan Trump did as he was instructed. Satisfied that the handcuffs were secure, Mannion ordered the outlaw to walk his horse until they were clear of the danger, but warned, 'Be ready to hit the trail, if those bastards put in an appearance.'

A woman's scream filled the still desert air. Mannion winced. It pained him to leave the women to their fate, but there was nothing he could do. There were at least twenty Apaches. Even if he'd been loco enough to try, the first thing the Indians would do was slit the nuns' throats. Considering what he'd witnessed, that would have been a relief to the women.

From Bony Ridge, Zacariah Trump watched keen-eyed as a passing band of Apaches made their way to the camp Hunting Wolf had set up, and to which all bucks were now making their way on the instructions in the smoke.

Jed Trump, seeing the frown of concern on his father's face, enquired of him, 'What's eatin' ya, Pa? Ain't nothin' for us to piss in our pants 'bout. 'Paches and us are a'most kin.' Enthusiastically he suggested: 'We could use their help in findin' Nathan and that lawman.'

Zachariah Trump kept his silence. He'd never told his sons about the dirty dealings he'd gotten up to, palming off useless rifles to Hunting Wolf. Guns that had cost the lives of ten bucks by either exploding or jamming, and had left Hunting Wolf himself carrying an ugly scar that dragged his right eye nearer his mouth than nature had intended. Two years had passed, but Zachariah knew that if he crossed paths with Hunting Wolf, he'd roast him like a hog over an open fire.

'Ya're surely troubled somethin' awful, Pa,' Jed Trump observed.

Zachariah had not confided in Jed and Frank Trump. He knew his sons well. If he had, they'd likely have not ridden with him.

Dusk was shading the desert sky with long streaks of purple and orange when Dan Mannion drew rein in a bowl of rocks which he hoped would keep his meagre fire hidden from prying eyes. His

progress through the long, scorching afternoon
had been slow and ponderous, and full of menace.
He had taken many risks, often pressing on when
he should have sought a hidy-hole. He knew that
he'd pushed his luck to the limit, and he fretted
about how much more good fortune was left to
him. Enough to see him through to Tuteville and
Rosie O'Sullivan's arms, he hoped.

A supper of beans and coffee ready, Mannion
immediately doused the fire, taking no chance on
its glow being seen as darkness deepened.

Shivering, Nathan Trump complained, 'Damn
it, Mannion. Might as well be sittin' in Rockies
snow. We need that fire.'

'Make do,' the marshal growled, in no humour
to listen to his prisoner's griping.

Supper over, Mannion draped a blanket round
his shoulders and settled back against a stunted
tree, holding his Winchester. It would be a long
night, with little if any sleep. The marshal
wondered about how much longer he could stay in
the saddle.

Rosie O'Sullivan woke cold and miserable to
begin another day of fretting. She had been avoiding town, not wanting to hear the speculation
about Dan Mannion's fate, and therefore her vigil
was a lonely one.

'If the Trumps don't skin him, 'Paches will for

sure,' seemed to be the general opinion about Dan's chances of surviving.

Judge Harding was already talking about an election for Dan's replacement.

'You should have confidence in your marshal to get the job done, Judge,' Rosie had berated Harding. 'Dan Mannion's the finest man I've ever had the pleasure of knowing, sir.'

Rosie's fiery rebuke had alerted folk to the true nature of her feelings for the marshal. From then on talk of Dan Mannion's fate was whispered when she was near.

'In heaven's name, Dan,' she wept. 'Have pity and come home.'

She got up, went downstairs to the kitchen and brewed coffee. Coffee, contrary to what Doc Bennett, Tuteville's medico claimed, always settled her nerves. She stood at the kitchen window, watching the grey fingers of dawn reach across the sky to grab the sun and lift it up. Her heart ached, fit to break. Rosie prayed that this would be the day when she'd again see Dan Mannion.

Hunting Wolf, too, was praying, in his own way to his own god. His special entreaty was for the deliverance of Zachariah Trump to him.

Zachariah Trump was not praying at all.

# FOUR

Rolling out of his blanket, Dan Mannion felt grimy with the dust of the trail on his skin and in his hair, thankfully thinner now than when he'd started toting a badge, and less likely to harbour the bugs that would abound in the desert. He'd have given a great deal at that moment to be able to visit the bathing-parlour which Rosie O'Sullivan had started up back in Tuteville. His thoughts rambled pleasantly back to his first visit to the parlour.

'You expect me to swish about in that?' Dan had asked Rosie, doubtfully eyeing the fancily painted tub, when she'd invited him to be her first customer on the parlour's opening day. 'Not sure if a man can remain respectable, scrubbing in something like that,' he'd opined. Figuring that he'd find it mighty difficult to cover the important parts of his six-feet-three frame.

His surprise had been even greater when, after bathing, Rosie had shaved him and doused his face with a fancy lotion.

'Comes from Paris, France,' she'd told him. That got Mannion wondering about Frenchmen.

'Dang it, Rosie,' he'd complained, on leaving the parlour, 'even my horse is giving me strange looks.'

'Stand right where you are, Dan Mannion,' Rosie had ordered. 'Let folk see your glow and smell your fragrance.'

'Heck,' an old-timer who lounged on the porch outside the hotel which was next door to Rosie's bathing parlour, cackled, 'you smell purtier than a saloon dove, Marshal.'

'Aw, Rosie,' Dan had protested, as folk had gathered round to sniff at him.

'What've you got to smile 'bout?' Nathan Trump asked grumpily.

Dan Mannion scowled at the interruption to his memories. He handed Trump a strip of jerky, which the outlaw threw back at him.

Dan shrugged. 'It isn't my gut that'll be rumbling, Trump.'

'Ain't you got bacon, coffee?'

'Bacon and coffee needs flame to prepare, and I'm not risking a fire this early. The air's too clear. A man's smoke has no competition.'

'It ain't goin' to make no diff'rence, Mannion. Might as well die on a full belly, I say.'

Dan resisted the killer's goading. Anger was an emotion that not only drained a man of vital juices, it also made him careless.

'Do I get water?' Trump growled.

'Nope. Later when the sun burns you'll get a mouthful. But that's all.'

To hide the worry in his eyes, Mannion turned his back on Trump. He had half a canteen of water, which was fouling fast. There was a water hole at a place called Lancome's Drift, a couple of miles east of where they were. The trouble was, water holes were where folk stopped to refresh themselves. That made them a natural hunting-ground for Indians seeking to add to their tally of scalps. Bad water would lay a man low. In the desert that was almost always fatal. But with Apaches on the prowl, and the Trumps on his tail, Mannion knew that such a misfortune would certainly bring about his demise. Another worry was that, if he diverted to Lancome's Drift, he would lose precious time in reaching the relative safety of Rourke's Trail. Sometimes there were pockets of water trapped in rocks and crevices, which might prove handy. The small wells of rain-water from the desert storms had saved many lives, when all hope seemed lost. But they took time and luck to find, and were often found dry or fouled. In the desert, time wasted could be the last minutes of a man's life.

Dan saddled the horses. The animals were weary and listless - pretty much spent. Trump read his thoughts.

'Ain't much more in them nags, Mannion.'

Dan wet his neckerchief and moistened the horses' mouths.

'Looks like them hollow-siders will fold, and you ain't goin' to make it back to that petticoat you've been moonin' 'bout.'

Dan recalled how Trump had sized him and Rosie up the morning he'd ridden into Tuteville, laughing on the boardwalk outside the law office. His quick-fire assessment of Mannion's feelings for Rosie O'Sullivan showed him to be a shrewd observer.

'Don't you worry none, though,' the outlaw chanted. His sneer was laden with evil menace. 'I'll surely drop by to visit. Rosie, ain't it, Marshal?'

Rounding on Trump, the marshal grabbed the outlaw by the shirt. He hauled him to his feet.

'You leave her name out of your filthy mouth, Trump. Or so help me . . .'

The bullet skewing off the rock nearest to Mannion had him diving for cover. He dragged Trump with him. A volley of shots quickly followed, none coming as close as the first, which made Mannion think that the shooters were not marksmen, and were counting on quantity instead of accuracy to achieve their goal. The first shot, Mannion decided, had been kissed by Lady Luck.

"Pache,' Trump cried triumphantly. Seeing his rescue at hand, he jumped up to show himself. 'I'm Nathan Trump,' he called out. 'I'm Zachariah Trump's youngest.' His glee turned to astonishment, when the Indians responded with more lead, forcing the outlaw to scurry back to cover. 'Don't understand,' he mumbled, genuinely puzzled by the response his declaration had received.

'Looks to me,' the marshal said, smugly, 'that your pa doesn't carry the kind of clout with the Apaches you were counting on, Trump.'

Dan looked to the boulders higher up from where the shooting had come, but thankfully they were not high enough to launch lead into the narrow crevice they'd taken refuge in. But neither could they break out without considerable risk, even with the Apaches' slipshod shooting.

Alarm replaced astonishment in Nathan Trump. 'They could pin us down here 'til we have beards to our toes, Mannion.'

'That's how it is, sure enough,' the lawman agreed.

The Tuteville lawman faced quite a dilemma. As his prisoner had said, the Indians could simply sit and wait, or some of them could creep up on

Mannion's hidy-hole under covering fire. His choices were: to stay put, or break from cover to reach the shale track which led up to the higher reaches where the Apaches lurked. Neither option was palatable, and either one would probably prove fatal. If he were to break for the track, it handed him another problem. Nathan Trump, handcuffed as he was, could not defend himself, and in Mannion's book every man, even a cur like Trump, had the right to defend himself in such a situation as they found themsleves in. But for the outlaw to defend himself, he would have to uncuff him, and give him a gun. The thought of Nathan Trump at his back, toting a gun, handed Dan Mannion the biggest worry of all. But what else could he do? A couple of hours in the blistering heat, more intense still in the cramped space of the crevice, would finish them both. In poor shape, due to lack of sleep and long hours in the saddle, Mannion had no illusions. His punished body was already getting heavily weary, and if he remained where he was for a while longer, his legs would become leaden and cramped, putting him in no fit state to sprint the distance to the shale track.

The path to the Indians would normally be treacherous and sapping. Under fire, it would be murderous. Dan saw another danger. Two of the Indians were working their way along the rim of the boulders, out of six-gun range, towards where the horses were. Mannion had no doubt but that their intention was to shoot the horses, and leave them stranded. Then they would wait and enjoy the death watch.

Dan ducked as another bullet probed the crevice, whining away like a demented banshee. Mannion made up his mind.

'We can't sit here frying. You'll have to cover me, Trump.'

The outlaw sneered. 'Cover ya? Ain't you 'fraid I'll shoot you in the back?'

'No.'

'Oh?'

Mannion said, 'Right now, until we're out of this bind, you need me as much as I need you, Trump.'

Trump chuckled. 'Ain't it surely strange how necessity makes for strange bedfellas, Marshal!'

# FIVE

Zachariah Trump cocked his ear.

'What, Pa?' Jed Trump asked.

'Gunfire.'

Frank Trump, sore-headed from the rotgut that he'd spent most of the night supping, said surlily, 'In your head, Pa.'

Zachariah called a hush and gave his full concentration to listening. He'd have sworn that he had heard the report of distant rifle-fire.

'In your head, Pa,' Frank repeated.

'Yeah,' Jed said, listening. 'Nothin', Pa.'

Zachariah sank back on his haunches to spoon beans into his mouth, thoughtful. Convinced of what he'd heard, he ordered, 'Saddle up.'

Frank pulled his blanket back over his head. Zachariah laid a boot on his rump.

'What'cha do that for?' Frank Trump growled.

'I said saddle up,' the Trump patriarch snarled.

Jed, who had been about to support his brother's protest, quickly changed his mind, not wanting to earn his father's anger, as Frank was doing more and more these days. In fact, only a week previously, Frank had hinted to Jed that he was thinking of forming his own gang. Jed was not opposed to the idea, but neither had he the courage to come out with outright support for the radical move. Sneakiness being Jed's prime characteristic, he would wait until the cards fell, and then pick the winning hand.

Zachariah and Frank Trump had always been at odds, but even more so since a month previously, when Frank's sloppiness in not instantly killing a bank teller during a bank raid, almost cost Zachariah's favourite, Nathan, his life when the teller, who proved to be no mean shot, had started blasting at them from the bank door. Zachariah, as mad as a riled mountain cat, had laid into Frank at the first opportunity after dodging the posse. Frank had angrily drawn iron on his father. The ugly confrontation had made the gap between them unbridgeable.

'Now!' Zachariah added, again threatening Frank with his boot.

'Get up, Frank,' Jed pleaded with his brother, as Frank Trump's defiance to Zachariah's prodding hardened.

Frank shot Jed a snarling look. 'Mind your

own damn business, Jed.'

'No call to talk to your brother that way,' Zachariah snapped.

Boosted by his father's support, Jed was set to continue his harassment, but Frank cut him down to size.

'Takin' orders from you is one thing, Pa,' he said. 'Takin' guff from Jed, I ain't. Any more gab,' he warned Jed, 'and I'll lay into ya.'

'That a fact?' Jed said hotly. He grabbed his gunbelt and buckled it on. His hand hovered over his gun. 'Wanna try, Frank?'

Zachariah watched the anger between his sons grow. It didn't bother him. Of the two, he'd prefer Jed to come out on top. Frank, he had always felt distant from.

'I just might at that,' Frank growled.

Zachariah had a mind to let his boys settle their differences there and then, and would have, only for the fact that he needed them both to fight off any challenge by the Apaches, or the lawman who had Nathan on tow on a rope. The Tuteville marshal was formidable opposition. He had to be, to have ridden into outlaw-infested territory to snatch Nathan, and since then to have survived the rigours and dangers of the desert.

'You boys settle down now,' Zachariah ordered. 'It ain't right for kin to be shootin' kin.'

Frank figured that the old man's lecture was a mite sanctimonious. At fifteen he'd shot down his own father in cold blood, when he caught him up to no good in the barn with his sister.

'I ain't takin' Frank's lip, Pa,' Jed raged.

'Then take mine,' Zachariah roared. 'And do as you're told.'

Jed thought about squaring up to his father, and would have, if he'd thought he had the beating of him. Zachariah could see inside Jed's head, and liked the evil he saw. The boy had the kind of spite in him that he'd had as a young man.

'That's an end to this bickerin'.' Zachariah's blazing eyes flashed from one to the other. 'You hear me?' he demanded.

'Sure, Pa,' they mumbled.

'Let's ride.'


As the latest volley of lead buzzed through the rocks, Dan Mannion knew that his luck could not last for ever. With hot lead buzzing all round him, it was only a matter of time before a stray bullet found its mark. He already had a stinging graze on his right cheek, caused by a stone chip, to remind him of how potentially deadly the Indians' fire was.

Cowering, Nathan Trump edgily challenged Mannion: 'You goin' to sit 'round all day?'

The truth was, Dan was finding it hard to hand

over a six-gun to the outlaw. To gain time, he hedged. 'I'm thinking.'

'Thinkin'?' Trump yelped, as more lead spun off the rocks around them. 'That'll be kinda hard to do with a hole in your head!'

Dan, resigned to the fact that he would have to take his chances on handing Trump a gun, did so, and geared himself for his sprint from cover. There was no alternative, so he might as well get on with it. Even if the Apaches did not get lucky with lead, the desert sun would do the job for them. Their cramped hidy-hole sizzled. They were, in fact, meat in an oven.

It was a miracle that the horses had not bolted, but the Indians creeping towards the animals would soon counter that miracle, and leave Mannion and Trump without mounts. Without horses it was certain that their bleached bones would be added to those of all the other souls the hostile and deadly environment had claimed.

The marshal uncuffed Trump, reminding the outlaw: 'Remember, if you're tempted to use that shooting-iron on me, it looks like the Apaches dislike you as much as they hate me.'

Dan Mannion flexed his leg muscles to improve his circulation, impeded by the cramped space in which he had been forced to take cover. Ready as he'd ever be, the marshal sprinted for the shale track, by which he planned to reach the Indians' higher-up lair, hoping that cramp would not hobble him.

Instantly, as he broke cover, bullets bit the ground all round him. As he ran, the Tuteville lawman wondered if one of the spraying bullets had his name on it.

# SIX

Alerted by hoofs in the yard, Rosie O'Sullivan ran to the front door. She yanked open the door, ready to fling herself into Dan Mannion's arms. She pulled up sharply on seeing Luther Barrett standing on her doorstep, proffering a bunch of flowers.

'Luther. What are you doing here?'

Her snappiness of tone had the rancher scowling darkly, his brown eyes smouldering angrily. Belatedly, Rosie added, 'You're surely welcome, Luther.'

'That a fact? Liar!'

'Luth —'

'Don't waste your breath, Rosie,' the rancher snapped. He looked sourly at the flowers. 'I bet if it was Mannion standing here, holding these, you'd be dancing a damn jig right now.' Rosie reached out to touch Luther Barrett's arm, but he pulled away in a sullen anger. 'Well, I guess I've got an answer without asking the question,

Rosie.' He snorted. 'Don't understand it. I can give you a palace, and all you want is a marshal's house.'

Rosie thought about trying to explain that it was the man and not the bank account that was important to her, but she held back on two counts. First, any attempted explanation would only cause further pain to Luther. The second reason she kept her powder dry was that she did not want to put Dan Mannion on the pedestal she figured he should be on, because Luther Barrett could cause Dan a whole lot of grief, should he choose to.

The rancher stalked off, shrugging aside Rosie's efforts to make amends. He swung into the saddle.

'Maybe,' he chewed, 'these will come in handy,' he flung the flowers across the yard, 'when Dan Mannion comes back boxed.'

Rosie gasped with the shock of Luther Barrett's vitriol, and she hated him from that second on. Angered by Luther Barrett's cruelty, Rosie grabbed a broom from the porch and laid its handle across the side of his head.

'Get out of my sight, Luther Barrett,' she raged. 'I don't ever want to see your ugly dial again!' In a black mood, Barrett nursed his head. 'Out of my sight,' Rosie repeated, again threatening the rancher with the broom.

41

Luther Barrett swung his mount and thundered out of the yard, taking out his temper on his unfortunate horse. He was a man of black moods, but as he galloped back to the Big B, he was in the blackest mood he'd ever been in.

During his breakneck journey back to the ranch, a poisonous seed took root in his tormented brain. On reaching the ranch house, he instructed a hand who grabbed the reins of the frothing stallion.

'Find Bellamy. Send him to the house. Now!'

The twenty seconds that it took Dan Mannion to cover the open ground to the shale path were the longest of his life. He was no stranger to danger, having faced an array of murdering honchos in his time as a lawman, but it was the uncertainty of the danger that now unnerved him. There was nothing he could do, only trust to luck as the Apaches above him rained lead on to the open ground. A quick diversion to grab a rifle from his saddle scabbard had almost proved fatal when a bullet had skewed off his saddle horn and buzzed the crown of his head. Half an inch lower and it would have taken the top of his head off. Maybe his luck was running good. He was still sucking air.

Dirt as hard as stones spat in Mannion's face, and jagged slivers of rock, prised loose from the boulders by the blistering hail of lead, spun about him, each particle a potential maimer. Mannion grimaced as a stone, gouged from the earth, caught the back of his left leg. Luckily it was blunt and stung more than damaged. If it had been a pointed missile it would have torn through muscle and ligament, and he'd have gone down. That would have been the end of him.

Nathan Trump had done the best he could with a six-gun, but, in reality, he might as well have been slinging pebbles at the Indians. Dan Mannion was conscious of the fact that the alliance between him and the outlaw was an unholy one, and that should circumstances swing in Trump's favour, he would not hesitate to use the Colt on him.

On reaching the track the marshal paused to draw breath, enjoying the cover that the looping curve of the track gave him. But it would be a temporary respite. Casting an eye up the track, Mannion could see stretches of it that were devoid of any cover, where he would be even more exposed than he already had been, and closer to the Apache rifles.

Not for the first time on this trip, he began to wonder if he'd see Rosie O'Sullivan again. Like any other man, Dan Mannion had a fear of dying. But his fear of dying was outweighed by the fear of not seeing again the woman who had become his reason for living.

A tomblike stillness descended. Dan had been hoping that hot-headedness on the part of the Apaches would hand him the advantage. But no advantage had been gained. The Indians knew the strength of their position, and seemed content to let the spider come to the fly.

Mannion's throat hurt with dryness. His eyes burned. Sweat rained off him like rainwater from a chute. He crept up the track, hugging what little cover there was, cursing as the sliding shale pinpointed his position all the way. His heart, constricted by the tension that had every nerve and muscle honed and ready for action, beat sluggishly.

He was forced under a narrow ledge by a sudden burst of gunfire. He held his breath and waited wide-eyed as a surprised rattler reared up, before sliding under a boulder. He knew that his encounter with the deadly snake could have gone either way, and hoped that his escape was yet another pointer to luck favouring him. Breathing again, Dan Mannion took in his surroundings. Where there was one rattler, there could be more. His search completed, without sight of further danger, he relaxed as best a man in his perilous straits could.

His relaxation was short-lived. Scree from

above him filtered down. He glanced up to see two gloating Apaches. Mannion's Winchester spat. His reaction had been quick. But had it been fast enough?

# SEVEN

This time there was no mistaking the sound of gunfire. Zachariah Trump's only problem was in detecting its source, its reason, and its avoidance if it did not concern him. The gunfire could have several reasons for breaking out. An Apache raid. A skirmish between hardcases. Or it could be to do with Nathan Trump and the Tuteville marshal. Whatever the reason, caution and stealth were called for.

'East, I reckon,' Frank Trump opined. 'A coupla miles.'

Jed Trump disagreed. 'South, I say.'

'Both of you shut your mouths,' Zachariah snapped. 'Let a man listen.' After a moment, he said, 'East. Less than a mile, I reckon.'

Dan Mannion felt the breeze of the Apache's bullet as the Indian toppled headlong from the ledge. Good fortune favoured the marshal. For the vital second he needed, the Indian's tumble unsighted his partner, giving Mannion the chance to shoot again. His second shot, though telling, was not fatal. The bullet nicked the Indian's left ear. In a blur of movement, the outraged Apache drew a wicked blade and defiantly hurled himself at Mannion, clearly intent on claiming the lawman's scalp in revenge.

The marshal's left leg, which had been injured in his sprint from cover minutes before, now buckled under him. His awkward stumble left him helpless. He glanced up, and it looked like he'd had his quota of luck. Knife poised, the Apache looked set to ram it to the hilt into Mannion's chest.

'You wanted to see me, Mr Barrett?'

Luther Barrett gulped down the remains of his third whiskey and slammed the glass down on his desk.

'Where the hell have you been, Bellamy?' he snarled. 'It's been over an hour.'

'North range,' the cold-eyed youngster said. 'Caught a rustler.'

'Rustler?'

'Not the kind you'd notice, Mr Barrett.'

'How many head?'

'Just one.'

'One?' the rancher exclaimed.

'A calf.'

Luther Barrett's eyes popped. 'A calf?'

'That dirt-poor sod-buster over near Walton's Creek.' His smile was as chilling as his icy-blue eyes. 'Hanged him.'

Barrett, though not a merciful man himself, was knocked back by Bellamy's action. 'You hanged a hungry man for stealing one calf?'

Bellamy shrugged. 'One . . . Hundred. Still rustling.'

A month previously, when Wes Bellamy was passing through Tuteville, Luther Barrett had seen him draw iron in the saloon. He'd been lightning-fast. Had Dan Mannion not stepped in, the man on whom Bellamy had drawn would certainly have paid the full price for his foolishness. Instinctively, and in defiance of the marshal's opinion, the rancher had hired the youngster, not knowing at the time what use he could put him to. He had just felt at the time that Wes Bellamy would one day have his uses. That day had now come.

'What is it you want me to do, Mr Barrett?' Bellamy asked in his distinctive Texas drawl.

Luther Barrett came straight to the point, feeling that he could put all his cards on the table with a man who had just hanged a hungry man for stealing a calf.

'Kill a man,' the rancher stated bluntly.

Bellamy grinned. 'Guess that's what you hired me for.'

Luther Barrett wondered if the Texan had hit the nail on the head. Had he always known, without admitting it to himself, that to gain Rosie O'Sullivan's hand, he'd one day have to dispatch Dan Mannion? Sometimes, he realized, a man knew things without being fully aware of those things, like the presence of the seed of murder in his heart.

'So, when do you want me to kill Mannion?'

The rancher was bemused. 'How . . .?'

Bellamy's grin widened in a knowing way. 'Figured it would come to this. Ain't no real call 'round here for my talents, other than dispatching the marshal.' The cocky Texan did not mince his words. 'Ev'ryone knows, that as long as the marshal is above ground, you ain't in the reckoning with Rosie O'Sullivan.'

Enraged, the rancher sprang from behind his desk to throttle Bellamy for his impudence, but he never got that far. The Texan's Colt in his belly brought him up short. The gunfighter sneered.

'Let's not have any unpleasantness . . . Barrett.' He forced the rancher back against his desk. 'What's the deal?'

'A thousand dollars. You leave when the job's done. I don't want to ever see you again.'

'Two thousand?'

'Two thou . . .! Fifteen hundred. Not a cent more.'

49

The Texan shrugged. 'I've killed men for less.'
He smirked. 'A whole lot less.'

Luther Barrett went to a wall safe hidden
behind a painting of a rearing mustang. He
counted out fifteen hundred dollars.

Flicking the bills, Bellamy said, 'What if I just
up and ride?'

Angered, Barrett flung back, 'I'll send someone
to find you. Someone faster.'

Bellamy scoffed. 'Faster?'

Luther Barrett said, 'There's always someone
faster, Bellamy. And if you don't believe that, I
reckon you're going to meet up with him sooner
rather than later.'

Bellamy scowled. 'What if the marshal don't
come back, Barrett?' Now that they were partners
in murder, the gunfighter saw no need to main-
tain a façade of respect for the rancher.

'You get to keep the money.'

'Mighty generous,' the Texan drawled. 'Reckon
it'll buy my silence, huh?'

Luther Barrett did not answer. There was no
need to. They both knew that the hired killer had
spoken the truth.

Now that he could not count on the Apaches as
friends, Nathan Trump waited anxiously for the
outcome of the tussle between Dan Mannion and
the Indian. The Tuteville marshal would take him

every step of the way to the hangman's rope waiting for him, but the Apaches would butcher him on the spot, or worse still, roast him slowly. With Mannion he stood a chance of avoiding that rope by maybe getting the drop on him. Unlike Mannion, the Indians would not be hindered by the rules of civilized behaviour. They'd rip his innards out and be done with it.

It had come as a numbing shock to the killer to find that Zachariah Trump held no sway with the Apaches. It was a development beyond his comprehension. Zachariah's dealing with the Indians had meant that he and his sons could roam freely and safely in Indian country. So what had changed?

The hunting knife flashed past Dan Mannion's face. The sun reflecting off the blade momentarily blinded him. Mannion rolled with the Apache, straining with the effort of holding off the ready-to-plunge knife. He managed to get his hand between the Apache's legs, and used the momentum of the roll to hoist him over and beyond him. The Indian crashed on to a boulder. The bone-jarring impact forced a gush of air from his lungs. Mannion had the advantage. He had to make it count. The Apache's pride had been dented, which made him doubly dangerous.

Now he'd fight to his last breath!

The marshal dived for the Indian and grappled with him. Out of the corner of one eye, he could see another Apache crouched on a ledge above him. Where had Nathan Trump got to? The Indian was within six-gun range. Had Trump made tracks?

His mobility was hampered by the earlier injury to his left leg, and he was finding it difficult to gain purchase on the Indian's greasy body, caked with putrefying animal fat that made him retch. The Apache slipped Mannion's hold. The Indian picked up a rock and threw it at the lawman. It bounced off Mannion's right shoulder. Shooting pain locked his neck muscles and his right hand was temporarily numbed. The Apache ducked under Mannion and got behind him. The Indian's arm encircled his neck, applying killing pressure. He forced the lawman round to face the second Indian poised on the ledge above him, rifle at the ready.

From his hidy-hole, Nathan Trump watched, undecided whether to help Mannion or make a break for it. How far would he get? Would his nag's legs last if the Apaches gave chase? Where could he go? Might he ride into even greater trouble? The outlaw's head throbbed. Not being a thinking man, the end result was total confusion. The killer opted for trying to save his own skin. He broke from cover, sprinting towards the horses.

The Apache on the ledge lined Dan Mannion up in his sights. Even though he was a lousy shot, the Indian could not miss. The Tuteville marshal knew that he had only seconds left to live.

# EIGHT

The woman who was occupying Dan Mannion's thoughts in his final seconds of life was riding across Barrett range, deeply troubled. Once her anger at Luther Barrett's visit had died down, Rosie O'Sullivan had decided that making it up with the rancher would be a whole lot better than having Luther as an enemy. Rosie was not too worried about herself. However, knowing Barrett's mean nature, she fretted that he could make trouble for Dan Mannion, once he was back in the marshal's chair. In the past, when riled, Luther Barrett had a spiteful and unforgiving nature, and there was no evidence that he had changed his spots. The Big B boss was the kind of man who was a generous friend, but a vengeful enemy should a man get on his wrong side. Rosie feared that by rejecting Luther for Dan Mannion, her action had put the marshal on Barrett's wrong side. It shouldn't have. But, angry, reason deserted Luther.

As she approached the ranch house, Luther spotted Rosie O'Sullivan through his study window, where he had taken refuge to assuage his guilt with liquor, after he had handed Wes Bellamy his task of murder. Elated by Rosie's appearance, and misinterpreting her visit, the rancher hurried to greet Rosie, as best his wobbly legs would allow him. Yanking open the front door, he exuberantly greeted his visitor.

'Rosie, darling. I knew you'd change your mind.'

Rosie's spirits slumped. As she had feared on the ride out to the ranch, Luther had taken the completely wrong meaning from her visit.

'Luth . . .' she began, but there was no shaking his conviction that she had changed her mind. He hoisted her from the saddle. His lips were on hers lightning-quick. She struggled to break free. He stood back from her, puzzled. On seeing Rosie's displeasure, his brow furrowed in anger.

'Luther —'

He waved aside what she had to say.

Exasperated, Rosie blurted out, 'Nothing's changed, Luther. I'm in love with Dan Mannion, and always will be, whether he'll have me or not.'

A dark anger contorted the rancher's face. 'Then what are you doing here?' he raged. 'Raising my hopes.'

'You raised your own hopes, Luther,' Rosie said, in a no-nonsense tone. 'I was hoping we could all be friends. Dan, me, and you.'

'Friends with Mannion,' the rancher howled. 'The man who stole you from me. Never!'

'Luther, please,' Rosie pleaded.

'Never,' Barrett repeated with a vicious snarl. He strode off.

Rosie O'Sullivan's heart sank to a new low.

Out in the desert, Mannion could not believe his eyes when the Apache's rifle exploded in the Indian's face. Stunned, the Apache holding him in a neck-lock relaxed his grip the slighest bit. But it was enough for the marshal to ram his elbow in the Indian's throat. The Apache stumbled backwards, grasping his throat and gasping for air. Mannion followed through with a kick to the groin that added greatly to the Apache's distress. The lawman grabbed his rifle from the ground, and shot the Indian dead centre of his forehead.

Another Indian, alarmed by the sudden change in fortunes, scurried up through the rocks, in his hurry throwing caution to the wind. Mannion put him in his rifle sights and dropped him. He turned in a low crouch. His rifle spat again. One of the Apaches making tracks towards the horses clutched at his chest, fell to his knees, and then on to his face. His partner fled, dancing as the Tuteville marshal's bullets bit at his heels. Mannion now swung his Winchester and put a pair of bullets in the ground in front of Nathan Trump, just as he reached his horse.

'One more step, Trump,' the lawman warned stonily, 'and you'll be buzzard-bait.'

Only a blistering couple of seconds had passed, but the cards had now fallen decisively in Dan Mannion's favour.

The outlaw dropped the reins he was holding, and raised his hands.

'Can't blame a man for tryin', Marshal.'

Dan Mannion came down the shale track, and crossed to where Trump was standing.

'No,' he agreed, 'you surely can't blame a man for trying.'

The marshal's easy, lopsided grin gave Trump no warning. Mannion's fist flattened the outlaw's nose, and sent him reeling backwards. Trump desperately tried to remain upright, but his legs, made hollow by the fury of Mannion's blow, buckled.

The Tuteville lawman came to stand over his prisoner. He chuckled. 'But bad boys have to be chastised for their misdeeds. Roll over on your belly,' he ordered. 'Hands behind your back.' He placed a boot on the outlaw's neck, bent down, and slapped handcuffs on him. 'Trump,' he grated, 'when're you going to get it through that dumb head of yours that you've got a date with the hangman, which I aim to see you keep.'

# NINE

Zachariah Trump's anxiety to avoid crossing trails with the Apache slowed the Trump trio's progress to a crawl. Zachariah's dithering drew questioning stares from Frank and Jed Trump. His jittery approach found empty terrain when they reached the scene of Dan Mannion's triumph.

Observing fresh blood, Jed opined, 'Nathan and that lawman can't be long gone from here, Pa.'

'If we hadn't been rock-dodgin' like we was, Pa,' Frank Trump said, critically, 'we'd have nailed that lawman.'

Uncharacteristically, Jed Trump showed backbone and added his criticism to his brother's, 'You ain't scared of a few 'Pache, are ya, Pa?' Jed enquired.

The senior Trump pointed angrily to a dust-trail, not far off. 'That ain't no few, timberskull. That there is a sizeable war party.'

'Makes no diff'rence t'us,' Frank Trump said. 'We're a'most kin to the 'Pache.'

Continuing in a defiant mood, Jed put in, 'Yeah. Why, they might even help us nail that damn Tuteville marshal, afore my ass is worn flat from straddlin' leather, Pa.'

Zachariah Trump wondered if he should tell them about his double-crossing of Hunting Wolf. Put them on guard that meeting up with the Apache renegade would not be good for any of their hides. Since setting out to rescue his son from the hangman's noose waiting for him back in Tuteville, Zachariah had had, because of his dirty dealing, to be careful not to alert the bloodthirsty Hunting Wolf to his presence. That caution explained how the Tuteville lawman had got so far with his prisoner. If Zachariah had had no worries about his own skin, he'd have long since sought the help of the Indians in running the lawman to ground. They'd pick up sign where no white man could see any. He knew his sons were beginning to wonder why he had not sought Apache help. The lawman called Mannion had pretty much given them the run-around up to now, whether by luck or intent.

The fact was that every minute was taking Mannion closer to Tuteville, and Nathan Trump's neck closer to a noose. Zachariah reckoned he had nothing to gain and everything to lose by telling

Frank and Jed of the threat to their skins from Hunting Wolf. He'd reared his boys in his own image, and that meant that it was more than likely that if they heard such unkindly news, they'd hightail it and leave him on his own to face Hunting Wolf. Even, he had no doubt, trade him for their own safety if needs be. Zachariah's gut knotted, as he contemplated the cauldron of danger which the desert had become. On setting out, he'd reckoned that tracking the lawman who had grabbed Nathan would be easy. However, the Tuteville badge-toter had proved to be a foxy opponent, and had drawn Zachariah into the desert further than he was comfortable with, with Hunting Wolf on the prowl. He had planned to hole up in Mexico until the cavalry put legs under the renegades, but the Tuteville marshal's arrival had scuppered that plan.

There was no doubt but that the dust-trail was stirred up by Apache ponies. The horses were being ridden too fast. Cavalry mounts had to be used sparingly. The Indians had no such problems, horse-flesh not being a commodity they were short of. The mountain valleys had an abundance of wild horses. The Apaches could ride their mounts to a standstill, because there were always a second and third string of ponies to call on. Another pointer was the weaving nature of the dust-trail, indicating that the riders knew every inch of the terrain over which they rode, inside out. The cavalry's progress would have been more cautious, with frequent stops to reconnoitre the country ahead, with consequent breaks in the dust-trail.

Frank Trump's question interrupted Zachariah's intense study of the dust-plume.

'Why're you frettin' so 'bout a few 'Paches, Pa?'

'I ain't frettin',' Zachariah snapped. 'Thing is, I don't want no hindrance to be put in the way of savin' your brother's neck. Now move!'

Frank grabbed his father's reins. 'Me and Jed's been talkin', Pa. Seems t'us that it ain't sensible not to ask the 'Paches for help. The way we've been meanderin', that marshal might be too far 'head for us to snare him.' Knowing Jed's slippery nature, Frank exchanged glances with his brother to check if he still had his backing. 'Fact is, Pa, Jed and me ain't never seen you sweat like you're sweatin' now.'

Zachariah Trump's anger-filled eyes bored into Frank Trump, making him cringe. But he figured that if he were to drop his challenge to the old man now, Trump senior would probably flay him alive for his impudence.

'Seems to me and Jed,' Frank went on, shakily, wilting under his father's malevolent glare, 'that you've been pickin' your way over the trails with the careful footin' of a greenhorn.'

'Yeah, Pa,' Jed said. 'Frank and me've been wonderin' 'bout that.'

The Trump patriarch growled contemptuously, 'If you boys're scared, then to hell with you both. Ride out right now!'

Zachariah turned his most hate-filled gaze on Jed Trump, figuring that his backbone would crumble easier than Frank's. He knew his sons well.

Jed whined, 'Mebbe me and Frank've been a tad rash, Pa . . .'

Frank fumed at Jed's back-stabbing climbdown. He'd been itching for a long time to challenge Zachariah Trump's supremacy, but he hadn't the guts to face the old man on a one-to-one basis.

Zachariah turned a sneering face Frank Trump's way. 'You thinkin', maybe, that your pa shouldn't ramrod this outfit, Frank?' he asked, in the soft tone which Frank knew meant awful danger.

Frank Trump's brief flirt with rebellion was sunk.

'Guess not, Pa,' he mumbled.

Zachariah drew his gun, and laid its barrel viciously across Frank Trump's face. Blood gushed from a raking gouge on his left cheek. 'Next time you buck me, Frank,' Zachariah Trump warned, 'I'll rip your tongue from its roots. You hear!'

'Sure, Pa,' Frank whimpered. But when he rode ahead, anger as hot as hell's coals burned in his eyes. Some day soon, he reckoned, the time would come for him to hold his ground against the old man.

As they rode on, Dan Mannion's body ached wearily. He could have done without the energy-sapping skirmish with the Apaches. Nathan Trump had become sullen and even more dangerous. He had never expected the Tuteville lawman to have survived so long. Where the hell were his kin? They were now his only hope of avoiding the hangman's rope. For some unknown reason, the Apaches had withdrawn their friendship, and seemed as ready to take his scalp as they were Mannion's.

The marshal reckoned that by nightfall, barring any other interruptions, and if his luck held, he would reach Rourke's Trail. For the impetus to go on, Dan Mannion turned his thoughts to Rosie O'Sullivan.

Ensconced in a mine shack in the gap at the end of Rourke's Trail, where he was betting on Dan Mannion riding through, if he survived the desert, Wes Bellamy rolled a smoke and settled down to wait. He figured that he had chosen his bushwhacker's lair wisely and well. The shack overlooked a narrow gorge, through which, if his thinking was right, Dan Mannion would ride on the final leg of his journey back to Tuteville. The alternative route was across flat, open country, where a fly couldn't travel without being spotted. Yes, he was certain that, with Apaches on the prowl, and the Trump brood dogging his tail, the marshal would opt for Rourke's Trail as his passage to town. That was, of course, if Mannion wasn't already buzzard-bait. He'd wait a couple of days. If Mannion had not put in an appearance by then, Bellamy reckoned that he could safely ride on – Dan Mannion would not be coming back.

He fingered the roll of bills in his vest pocket, and sighed contentedly. Down Mexico way, or perhaps further on, say Peru or Honduras, 1500 dollars, if he were to use it wisely, could make a man a king. Bellamy had already planned on adding significantly to his wealth by opening a brothel and saloon. There was always money to be made in sex and liquor. Another string to his bow would be gun-running. In countries where revolution was endemic, there was always a healthy profit to be turned from arms trading.

He chuckled. Sex. Liquor. Guns. Yes, sir. He was going to be a wealthy man: a very wealthy man indeed. He drew the smoke from his quirly deep into his lungs, and let it slowly trickle down one nostril. He picked up a bullet from the grime-laden table and rolled it between his fingers.

'This, Marshal Mannion, sir,' he murmured, and slotted the bullet into the Winchester's breech, 'is for you.'

# TEN

As they came out of the gully that Mannion had been using as cover, he saw circling vultures. It did not take long after that to find the burned wagon and three charred and half-devoured bodies; a man, a woman, and a little girl. Though time was running against him, he covered the remains with rocks, while listening to Nathan Trump's continuous bitching about it not mattering a fig.

'There's a hun'red an' one critters who'll have them uncovered in no time at all.'

'Shut your mouth,' Mannion bellowed. 'Or so help me, you'll lie here too, Trump.'

Ragged at the edges as Dan Mannion was, the outlaw stopped his whining. It took an hour to finish the makeshift graves, and it was an hour in which the evening darkened rapidly under storm-clouds racing up from the south.

'We'd best head for Hannigan's Reach,' Nathan

Trump advised. 'When that storm breaks there won't be an inch of this hell-hole desert safe from lightning. Flash floods, too.'

Mannion had to concede the wisdom of Trump's reasoning. Even if he pressed on to Rourke's Trail now, it would likely be a raging river of mud and shale by the time he reached it – if he reached it.

'Hannigan's Reach?'

'A trading post,' the outlaw informed Mannion.

'Out here?' the marshal asked sceptically.

'Ain't as loco as it seems,' Trump said. 'Lots of roosts round here. Hannigan catered to their needs. Women, whiskey, grub, ammo, horses. Stretch Hannigan wasn't the fool folk reckoned he was when he started the post a coupla years back.

'First day Hannigan arrived at where he was to put down roots, he rode straight into the hills and found the nearest Apache village to parley with them. Figured that if he was going to lose his scalp, he might as well lose it afore he hauled lumber and dug a well.

'The Indians, stunned by this white man's daring, took to thinking that Hannigan was favoured by the gods. Left him 'lone after that. In fact, much to some folks 'noyance, Apaches became regular visitors to the post.'

Dan Mannion looked to the storm-angry sky. 'How far is this Hannigan's Reach?'

'A coupla miles east.'

Trusting the killer did not rest easy with Mannion. Trump could be leading him straight into a trap. But, he figured, it was a matter of balancing risks. Stay in the open desert and risk the dangers of the storm, which would be considerable. Or head for Hannigan's Reach and relative safety, he hoped.

'Whatever way you call it, Marshal,' Trump said smugly. 'You ain't goin' to have it easy 'tween here and Tuteville.'

Dan Mannion did not need Trump to draw him any pictures. He was only too aware of the dangers all around from nature and man. He was near exhaustion. His sleep had been fitful, always with one eye on the wily Nathan Trump, who was ever ready to pounce on the least opportunity to get free of his shackles, by whatever means it took. His head was lead-heavy. At times the desert terrain was lost in a red haze. His tongue crowded his mouth, swollen from thirst.

Nathan Trump was in much better shape. Ten years Mannion's junior, with the advantage of having spent long spells in the desert hiding out, had put him in a lot better state to withstand the rigours of the harsh terrain and blistering heat.

Over the last few hours, Trump had watched Mannion as a hungry vulture might a tasty meal, waiting for him to keel over. Then he'd slit his throat and ride back across the Rio to finish what he'd started with the Mex whore, before Dan Mannion's untimely interruption.

Nathan Trump was growing in confidence now that he'd slip the noose waiting back in Tuteville for him. Who knew what might happen at Hannigan's Reach. Stretch Hannigan would be only too aware that if he failed to help him, Zachariah's revenge would be swift and deadly.

'Guess it's Hannigan's Reach,' Mannion decided. As they rode off, the Tuteville lawman warned his prisoner, 'Just keep in mind, Trump. The first sign of trouble, and you're a deadman.'


Hunting Wolf knew that time was short now. In another day or two he would have to flee to Mexico to avoid the horse-soldiers whom his scouts had sighted. But before they came, he would slit many throats and take many paleface scalps; like the scalps of the funnily dressed white women that his braves had crossed paths with the day before, and who had a god that no one could see; a god called Jesus.

Hunting Wolf had heard of these women visiting the reservations. He had heard of his brothers giving up ancient ways to follow this Jesus. But he would not! He was Apache. A proud hunter and fierce warrior. He would fight until the Apaches stood tall and proud again. The white-eyes would tremble at his name. He would make the vultures fat with the white man's flesh.

Mannion had been watching Hannigan's Reach trading post for over an hour, without seeing any sign of life. A wagon, its canvas ripped, stood outside the trading post. Behind the post, as far as he could see, the corral was empty. That dashed any hopes he had of finding fresh horses. It could be cavalry or Indians who had commandeered the horses Hannigan traded in. A woman's bonnet lay on the ground, half-way between the post and the wagon.

Nathan Trump said grumpily, and not for the first time, 'There ain't no one there, I tell ya.'

Still, Mannion waited. Apaches were a patient breed. The storm had veered off, and a tailwind had blown up. The marshal welcomed its cooling balm on his scorched skin. But soon the sun would vanish, and the balmy breeze would become a chilling wind. That was the thing about the desert. It was as hostile cool as it was hot.

How long would he wait? He'd have to make a move some time. He might as well make it now. Nightfall could work for or against him.

'Walk your horse,' the lawman ordered his prisoner. 'Keep blind side of it.'

Walking in a crouch, Mannion led off. He had a

sense of watching eyes. But in the circumstances he was in, a man's imagination could play all sorts of cruel tricks on him. Tricks? He hoped.

# ELEVEN

Luther Barrett was pacing his study when Lew Cohen, his ramrod, entered.

'Well?' the rancher asked anxiously.

Cohen shrugged. 'Seems Bellamy's vanished into thin air, Mr Barrett.'

'Keep searching for him,' Luther ordered brusquely.

'Yes, sir.'

'Take more men if you need them.'

'We're pretty stretched as it is —'

'Do it!'

Cohen, used to his boss's tantrums simply nodded and left. Why Wes Bellamy had suddenly become so all-fired important was none of his affair. He put in his time and drew his pay. So he might as well put it in searching for Bellamy as looking up the rear end of cows.

Luther went to the study window to watch his

foreman lead off a dozen riders. As was not uncommon, once the rancher's anger died down, he often viewed his actions with a more moderate eye. He had let his fury over Rosie O'Sullivan's rejection scatter his wits, and he now bitterly regretted having handed Wes Bellamy the task of murdering Dan Mannion. Not that he didn't hate the marshal's guts. He'd done that since the first time he'd seen Rosie fawning over him.

His plan had been simple. Have Bellamy kill Mannion. Then he'd step in to comfort Rosie. Later, when her grieving was over, there would be no obstacle that he could see, to Rosie becoming Mrs Luther Barrett. But as his anger cooled, he began to realize that, if his plan worked, he'd have to spend his life with Rosie harbouring a most awful secret; a secret that she could discover at any time. Sure, Bellamy would hightail it after his deed. But it was in the nature of secrets to reveal themselves sooner or later. A careless word. An overheard snippet. Simply two and two put together. How could he be happy with Rosie with the sword of Damocles hanging over him?

He'd have to rein in Bellamy. If he could find him . . . .

As Dan Mannion closed the gap on Hannigan's Reach, his every nerve was alert. His ears were pricked for the slightest sound. A rustle of cloth. A gun being primed. An intake of breath. A cough. But there was nothing.

Wait.

Mannion listened. The buzz of flies. He honed in on their source, a stunted tree. He approached the tree in carefully measured steps. When he rounded it, his guts spilled what little they had in them. Even the killing-hardened outlaw spewed.

'Hannigan?' the lawman asked.

'That's Hannigan,' Nathan Trump gagged, 'I guess.'

The trading-post owner's skull had been split open. Gorging flies filled the wound, as they did Hannigan's mouth where his tongue had been ripped from its roots. His belly, too, had been sliced open, offering the flies another feast. His eye sockets were empty, and there was a gaping hole on the right side of his face. His bootless feet were burned. Stretch Hannigan had dipped into the well of luck once too often, and had died hard for his impudence.

Feeling the chill of eyes on his back, Mannion suddenly turned his attention to the trading post. This time it was not his imagination at work.

'There's someone watching us,' he murmured to Trump.

The outlaw was doubtful. 'We'd have been cut down long 'go.'

'Maybe.'

When he spoke, Nathan Trump's voice was laced with raw fear. 'We could make a bolt for it.'

'Not on these horses,' Mannion said.

'We just can't stand here,' Trump panicked.

'Guess not,' the marshal agreed.

'What the hell do we do?'

Mannion said grimly, 'Take our chances, I guess.'

Mannion strode towards the trading post.

'You loco?' Nathan Trump whined.

The marshal reasoned, 'If we turn tail, we won't stand a chance. Might as well try and brazen this out.'

As he drew near the post, through the open door Mannion saw a scalped woman. That explained the bonnet, he figured. Further along, draped across the counter, face down, was another woman. Her hitched-up skirts and lower naked-ness, was clear evidence of how she had been used before being butchered. The sweet, sickly stench of death made breathing difficult.

Coming to stand alongside Mannion, Nathan Trump was relieved. 'Nothin' here 'cept ghosts.'

The bullet that clipped the outlaw's hat from his head sent them diving for cover, either side of the trading-post door, just as a second bullet tore a chunk of wood from the doorframe. Flat-backed and breathless against the wall, Dan Mannion gave calculated consideration to the shooter's skill, or lack of it. The two rifle shots had been close enough to indicate gun-slickness. However, if the purpose was to kill them, why engage in Fancy Dan antics like blowing off Trump's hat? Unless that was a lucky shot, of course? Fancy shooting? Or wild shooting? Their luck? A marksman giving warning? Or a shaky amateur?

There was only one thing Dan Mannion was certain of – the shooter was not Stretch Hannigan.

'What now?' Trump asked breathlessly.

'Now,' Dan said, 'we have to root out that shooter.'

'Root him out?' the outlaw bleated. 'You saw that shootin' just now.'

'Yeah. And I'm betting that it had a whole lot of luck to it.'

'That a fact!'

'I reckon,' Dan said.

'What if you're wrong?'

The Tuteville marshal said dourly, 'Then, my friend, I'll catch lead, and you'll be left with a mighty big problem.'

'Ain't ya got nothin' to live for?' Trump barked.

An image of Rosie O'Sullivan's lovely face floated in front of Dan Mannion's eyes. 'More than I ever had,' he said.

Resigned, the outlaw asked, 'So, what's the plan?'

'Simple. You create a diversion while I charge inside.'

'What kinda diversion?' Trump asked shakily.

'You'll have to draw fire, to give me time to get through the door.' Sweat as thick as axle grease oozed from Nathan Trump's pores. 'The way I see it,' Dan drawled, 'we're both taking risks. You, when you break cover to draw fire. Me, when I get inside the post.'

Trump's courage was as thin as tissue paper. His face was ashen.

'We're in a bind,' Mannion reminded the killer. 'If we break for our horses, we're dead, I reckon. So the only option open to us, that I can see, is to root out the shooter.'

Nathan Trump's mean, pebble-eyes glowed with the idea that had just come to him. 'I'll help. But only if you'll let me ride when this shindig is over with?'

'Can't do that,' Mannion replied flatly. 'You murdered a Tuteville citizen. You're going to stand trial for it.'

Figuring that he was holding a winning hand, the outlaw crooned, 'Makes no diff'rence to me if I die here, or at the end of a rope back in Tuteville, Marshal. But you've got that woman back in Tuteville you've been moonin' 'bout '

Dan Mannion nodded in agreement. 'The thing is, Trump, maybe you'll never see Tuteville?

78

Maybe you'll get the drop on me? Maybe your pa and brothers will catch us up? Maybe . . .? He chuckled. 'Lots of maybes.' Mannion's eyes bore into the outlaw's. 'Take a chance now, and, down the line, one of those maybes might happen. The alternative is to sit here until we fry, starve, or dry up.'

Nathan Trump's eyes darted about like a rattler's fang. 'Ain't much of a choice,' he growled, sourly.

'Better than you deserve,' the Tuteville marshal said, unsympathetically.

Wiping the lather of perspiration from his face, the outlaw said, 'Count of three?'

'Count of three,' Mannion agreed.

Jed and Frank Trump sat leather uneasily, concerned by Zachariah's uncharacteristic nerviness.

'What's eatin' the old bastard?' Frank asked his younger brother Jed. 'He's as jitt'ry as a hen with a coyote on the prowl.'

'He ain't been the same since that squaw flung herself off that canyon,' Jed opined. 'Pinin', I reckon.'

Frank Trump's scepticism was total. 'Pinin'? Pa?'

Jed Trump said, 'Well, what other explanation have you got, brother?'

Frank shrugged. 'Don't know, Jed. But I can't see Pa pinin' over no filthy 'Pache squaw.'

'Then tell me why he's wanderin' so?' Jed Trump growled argumentatively.

Frank shrugged again. 'Sure is a myst'ry, Jed.'

'What're you boys whisperin' 'bout?'

Frank and Jed Trump wilted under Zachariah Trump's satanic glare.

'Ain't nothin', Pa,' Frank said, hurriedly.

Zachariah Trump's fiery glare settled on Jed Trump. 'Jed. You wanna tell me 'bout your whisperin'?'

'Like Fr – Frank sa – said, Pa . . .'

Zachariah's stare intensified with the anger building in him.

'Well, Frank and me was thinkin' that since that squaw jumped off that canyon, you ain't been the same.' Seeing Zachariah's scowl lighten, Jed sniggered and got bolder. 'We was figurin' that you might be missin' your rations, Pa. Ain't that so, Frank.'

Zachariah was relieved that nothing more than dirt was churning through their heads. The last thing he needed on their part was intelligent thinking.

The Trump patriarch's wink was wily. 'Smart fellas, ain't ya.'

'Hell, Pa,' Jed said, relieved that the old man's fearsome temper was in abeyance, 'no need to fret so. The next squaw we cross paths with, Frank and me will snare her just for you.'

He chuckled. ' 'Preciate it boys.' Zachariah Trump had Wild Flower on his mind all right, but not in the way his sons reckoned. Besides trading Hunting Wolf dud rifles, he was witholding information from Frank and Jed which would make their deaths painful and slow, should Hunting Wolf get his hands on them. It was the knowledge that Wild Flower, the squaw whom they had all liberally enjoyed, was Hunting Wolf's only sister. Zachariah said with bonhomie, 'You boys ain't easy to fool, now are ya?'

Relaxed, Frank and Jed laughed along with him. Zachariah used the humorous interlude to fall behind to scan their back-trail and hide the apprehension in his eyes. Now there were several converging dust-trails. It looked like whatever direction he took, the devil would ride with him, laughing all the way.

Dan Mannion's breathing sounded like thunder to his ears as he waited in the dark hall for the shooter inside the trading post to make a move. He counted his time in seconds, every one more precious than the last. He called out, 'No need for anyone to die here.' His words were met with silence. Mannion reasoned, 'You might kill me. But then I might kill you . . .' He waited. Nothing.

'All I need is a canteen of water and some grub.'
He waited another spell before saying stonily,
'OK. Let's you and me take our chances, if that's
the way you want it. I've not got time to parley
more'

A door to the right of the hall opened slowly. A
gaunt-faced nun showed herself, Winchester
levelled at Mannion. Surprise dropped the
marshal's jaw. He holstered his Colt as a show of
good faith, and the nun dropped the rifle in relief,
sagging into Dan's arms in a faint.

Nathan Trump's face showed surprise every bit
as vivid as Dan Mannion's had been, but for an
entirely different reason. He clamped his lips
tight and kept his secret, pondering on how best
his secret might work to his advantage.

Mannion had been hoping for fresh horses at
Hannigan's Reach, but he would have to do with
the hollow-siders they had, which meant that his
progress to Rourke's Trail would be more
measured than he'd planned. In the desert, a slow
horse was better than no horse at all.

As they set out from Hannigan's Reach, riding
north to Rourke's Trail, Dan viewed the barren
country ahead with foreboding. If spotted, they'd
have little choice but to make a run for it. With
cover on the route to Rourke's Trail sparse, the
coming hours would be fraught with danger.
Progress would be ponderously slow. Their horses,

including the knock-kneed nag that Sister Lucy was on board, would buckle under them, should they have to bolt. Making a stand was not an option.

With Tuteville coming ever nearer, Nathan Trump would grab the slightest opportunity to avoid the waiting rope. With a woman in tow, the party became even more attractive for Apache attention. And where were the Trumps? Their whereabouts intrigued Dan Mannion. He had hoped to outrun them. However, with his trail obstacle-strewn, he'd have expected them to show before now. Which meant that they could put in an appearance any minute.

Sister Lucy had explained how it had been a miracle that she had not been killed by the Apaches. On the instructions of her reverend mother, she had been in the corral looking Hannigan's horses over, when the Indians had attacked the trading post.

'I hid under tarpaulin in an outhouse,' she'd explained.

Nathan Trump had smirked impudently. 'A true miracle, huh, Sister?'

'Indeed, sir,' Sister Lucy had replied uneasily, her eyes flitting in the marshal's direction. 'It was by God's grace that I was saved.'

'Surely was, Sister,' Trump had said wryly. 'The Lord truly works in wondrous ways.'

Mannion had pondered on the outlaw's familiarity, on Sister Lucy's discomfort, and, on the murmured conversation they had been engaged in just before leaving Hannigan's Reach. What would a nun and a killer have to talk about? He was at a loss to understand the tone of the exchanges between Nathan Trump and Sister Lucy. And finding a reason for the outlaw's wryness and sudden feistiness of spirit baffled the marshal.

For Trump's part, his being privy to a secret which he reckoned would have him escape a hangman's noose gave him a lot to be amused and light-hearted about.

Mannion was of a mind to chastise Trump for his disrespectful attitude to a woman who'd risk her skin trying to bring Christianity to the heathen Apache. But he held his tongue. The last thing he needed was more trouble.

# TWELVE

Dan Mannion rode away from Hannigan's Reach, counting the blessings which had been heaped on him up to now, and pondering the twists in the tail that might surprise him yet. Back in Tuteville, Rosie O'Sullivan had her worries, too. Following a trail of rumours, she caught up Luther Barrett's foreman, Lew Cohen, in the Double Diamond saloon. As she entered the watering-hole, all eyes went Rosie's way. Women in the saloon, other than doves, were a rare sight, and ladies of Rosie O'Sullivan's calibre not at all.

'Lost your way, Rosie?' the roly-poly Swede who owned the Double Diamond enquired, instantly offering Rosie his protection.

'Came to talk with Lew Cohen,' she informed the Swede.

'Me?' Cohen asked, stunned.

'Yes. Privately,' Rosie emphasized.

'At your service, ma'am,' Cohen said respect-fully. The Big B ramrod escorted Rosie to an out-of-earshot table at the far end of the bar. 'What can I do for you, Rosie?'

'You can tell me why you're so all-fired up look-ing for Wes Bellamy, Lew.'

Cohen shrugged. 'Don't rightly know.'

Rosie's brow furrowed in doubt. 'Don't know?'

'Nope. Mr Barrett tells me find Wes Bellamy, I find him pronto, Rosie.' He chuckled. 'Only it ain't pronto. Bellamy seems to have vanished into thin air.'

'Bellamy's a gunfighter, isn't he?'

The Big B ramrod shrugged. 'Seen one or two in my time. Bellamy sure's got the stance and atti-tude.'

'Why would Luther Barrett be looking for Bellamy so urgently?'

Cohen looked vague. 'Mr Barrett pays Bellamy's wages. I guess he's got the right, Rosie.'

'Yes, Luther pays his wages. Therefore, Wes Bellamy should be where Luther told him be,' she reasoned. 'So why is he turning every rock trying to find him, if Bellamy should be where Luther told him be, Lew? Doesn't make sense.'

'Sure don't.' The Big B foreman ran a hand over his stubbled chin. 'Rosie. Mebbe you should ask your questions of Mr Barrett, if you want right answers instead of my guessing.'

Rosie O'Sullivan stood up, her cheeks blazing with anger. 'You're right, of course, Lew. I'll do that right now!'

On the bend of a trail through a rocky gorge, a sextet of Apaches led by Summer Cloud, Hunting Wolf's confidant, unexpectedly clashed with the Trumps. There was a black hole where Summer Cloud's right eye had been, prior to one of Zachariah Trump's dud rifles exploding in his face. The Apache's malevolent glare dropped the temperature of Zachariah Trump's blood to zero. To Frank and Jed Trump's astonishment, Zachariah instantly wheeled his horse and galloped back through the gorge.

'What the dev —?'

Jed Trump's exclamation was cut short by a volley of shots buzzing around him. An arrow sliced his right cheek. Frank Trump, quicker to react, grabbed his brother's reins, and hauled Jed with him as he took off after Zachariah. His brotherly concern did not last for long when his own skin became increasingly endangered.

'Grab the damn reins, Jed,' Frank shouted, throwing the reins to Jed to catch as saving his own hide became his priority. Frank Trump's pistol flashed and the Indian nearest to him, tomahawk raised to split his skull, toppled from his pony.

'Start shootin',' he commanded his younger brother.

By now Zachariah had gathered his wits, but his bucking horse ruled out marksmanship. His bullets went wild. Frank's bullets were kissed by luck. Summer Cloud grabbed his chest, at the same second a hunting knife flashed from the Apache's right hand. Frank ducked low in the saddle. The knife whizzed harmlessly past, but found a target in Jed. Jed Trump grabbed at the knife in his windpipe, his eyes wild. 'Pa,' he croaked, before crashing from his horse. Jed triggered his six-gun in a reflex action, but, as he fell backwards, it only served to blow off the top of his own head.

Zachariah Trump aimed for the young buck charging towards him, fumbling with an unfamiliar Winchester, and blasted him clear of his pony. Frank triggered his Colt again, and another Indian fell.

With the odds on claiming Zachariah's and Frank Trump's scalps dramatically shortened, the remaining Indians, swift as mountain cats, wheeled their ponies in the tight confines of the gorge with the kind of horsemanship that only an Apache could master, and rode back into the rocks before Frank could get a clear shot at them. Hotheaded with temper, he gave pursuit, but Zachariah's restraining hand grabbed Frank's reins.

'Those bastards killed Jed,' Frank roared angrily.

'Nothin' we can do 'bout that,' Zachariah retorted harshly. 'Ain't no point in you and me followin' Jed to Hades!' Frank reined in his ire. The old man was talking sense. 'We gotta put trail 'tween us and those blood-lustin' savages. Pronto. Where there's one Apache, there's more that ain't far behind.'

Frank Trump's angry eyes went to where his kid brother lay, dead eyes looking to the desert sky.

'Ain't we goin' to bury Jed, Pa?'

'What for? His grave will only be rooted up by some critter anyway.'

'Don't seem proper to —'

'Ride, Frank!' Zachariah Trump ordered. 'No point in bein' weepy-eyed at a time our necks are in peril.'

Frank rode, but reminded his father, 'We got some talkin' to do, Pa. Soon. Real soon.'

Sister Lucy's mount was the first to buckle. The task of relieving the gelding's misery fell to Mannion. Being an animal-loving man, he shuddered as blood gushed from the horse's slit throat. A bullet in the head would have been kinder, quicker, and more merciful. But the explosion of sound in the desert stillness would

alert any interested parties to their whereabouts.

The threatening storm continued with its
fickle shenanigans, moving off, curling back,
only to move off again. The air weighed heavy,
trapping the furnace heat coming off the desert
floor. Breath could only be taken in short gasps.
Lungs burned. Muscles ached. Shoulders
drooped. Spirits dropped. With each gruelling
moment, as their progress became more and
more listless, Dan Mannion feared that, of all
the dangers surrounding them, it would be the
desert that would finally claim Sister Lucy and
him. Nathan Trump, a younger man, used to the
scorching climate, was handling the desert's
torture best. As Mannion's energy flagged, he
waited, biding his time, like the vultures
circling above them. The Tuteville marshal
looked to the sky's creeping darkness with hope.
A downpour would bring problems, sure enough.
But it would also bring relief and renewal. The
air would cool. The furnace inside his lungs
would be calmed.

The marshal also fretted about the nun's safety,
should her protection fall to Nathan Trump. To a
man like Trump, a woman was a woman, plain
and simple. Since leaving Hannigan's Reach,
Mannion had observed the outlaw's salacious
glances at Sister Lucy. Trump's eyes reflected the

filth churning in his mind. Even with the loose folds of a nun's habit, there was no hiding Sister Lucy's shapely form. Mannion knew that being a nun would not help her any. In fact, he suspected, her being a nun would act as a spur and not a deterrent to the murdering outlaw. Rape was just another foul quirk in Nathan Trump's demonic nature.

'You'd best ride with me, Sister,' Dan suggested coyly, embarrassed by the thought of having her arms clenched about his waist.

'My horse has got more grit left,' Trump said. 'Yours is pretty much spent, Mannion. Don't reckon that its back will take the extra weight.'

Trump was right. Mannion's horse was already wobbly-legged. Over the last couple of miles, there were a few times when the mare could have folded. That it hadn't was down to the marshal's horsemanship. Adding Sister Lucy's weight to his would greatly lengthen the odds against the horse holding out until the relative safety of Rourke's Trail was reached.

'The Sister can ride with me,' Trump proposed.

It made sense. Trump's animal, a feisty stallion, was in better shape. But the Tuteville marshal stated flatly:

'Don't reckon that's a good idea.'

Trump smirked cockily. 'How long d'ya reckon that nag of yours will last totin' extra weight,

Marshal? Don't seem sensible to me that you should reject my offer.'

Dan was stumped. It would be mule-headed to chance losing another horse. Little as he liked the idea, he had no choice other than let Sister Lucy share Trump's horse.

'You get up to any shenanigans,' he warned the outlaw. 'I'll drop you where you stand. Understood?'

Trump leered. 'Just hope you can keep them pretty hands to yourself, Sister.'

Unfazed by Trump's leering dial, Sister Lucy wasted no time in sharing Nathan Trump's saddle. Going stony-faced to his own mount, Dan Mannion wondered about the nun's lack of concern at sharing a saddle with any man, let alone a man of Nathan Trump's low character.

As they rode on, the saucer-sized raindrop which hit Mannion on the forehead spread relief across his scorched, tight skin. The sky was becoming as dark as Hades' dungeons. Distant lightning streaked like rivers of silver across the sky. Dan Mannion's relief at the prospect of the rain's cooling balm was counter-balanced by his worry that the impending deluge would also wash out Rourke's Trail. It was a steep, meandering track through wooded slopes. A downpour would loosen mud and shale. Sudden gushers from abandoned mines could sweep a man right off the track. He had ridden Rourke's Trail a couple of times over the years, and knew it to have an unpredictable and often cruel nature. The trail was in high, windswept country, and was subject to all the vagaries of weather. Old trails vanished. New trails opened up. All trails, new and old, had to be ridden a couple of feet at a time. Dan Mannion knew that, even if he reached and negotiated Rourke's Trail safely, a clear passage through the rocky gap that led down to Tuteville was not guaranteed. It was subject to landslides and, at the best of times, passage through it was precarious.

The marshal was counting on the Apaches not following him on to Rourke's Trail. Time must now surely be running against the Indians. The renegades had been raiding for almost two weeks. By now the army must be biting at their tails. Mannion reckoned that soon, if not by now, the Apaches would be fleeing back to Mexico for safe refuge. But the Apache did not always do what was expected of them. However things would pan out with the Indians, Dan Mannion was certain of one thing. Nathan Trump's kin would follow him right to Tuteville.

Hunting Wolf listened to his brave's report about his skirmish with the man called Zachariah.

'The one who traded guns possessed by devils.

He is not far away. In the place of faces.' The brave was referring to the gorge in which they had encountered the Trumps. At its entrance stood rocks with the shape of faces etched into them by eons of rain, wind, and sand.

There was another brave reporting, too. Three white-eyes, at the place they call Hannigan's Reach. The woman dressed like a crow. Like the women they had killed the previous day. 'The ones who talk about their invisible god,' the brave finished.

Hunting Wolf was pleased. It was better news than a scout had brought him a half-hour earlier about the long column of horse-soldiers. Before he fled to Mexico, he would teach the white man one final and terrible lesson. He would slaughter the one called Zachariah Trump and his kin. Then, the same fate would befall the white-eyes who had left Hannigan's Reach.

# THIRTEEN

Luther Barrett averted his gaze from Rosie O'Sullivan's.

'Tell me, Luther,' she demanded, fierily. 'Tell me what devil's scheme you've thought up for Dan Mannion. And what part Wes Bellamy is playing in that scheme.'

Barrett bluffed. 'Don't know . . .'

Rosie drew a Colt .45 from under her coat. Luther Barrett's eyes popped.

'You tell me right now,' she threatened. 'Or in a couple of seconds from now you'll be wormbait, Luther. That I promise you.'

After his initial surprise, the Big B boss gathered his wits together. He snorted, 'You're not going to shoot me, Rosie.'

The bullet that whizzed past him to blast a chunk of wood from his fine desk, inches from his left hip, had Barrett thinking again.

Rosie warned, 'I mean what I say, Luther. Now talk. And make it fast!'

A couple of hands, alerted by the gunfire, burst through the study door, guns drawn. Rosie O'Sullivan calmly swung the Colt their way and shattered a door panel.

'Vanish,' she ordered the two stunned men.

They glanced to their boss.

'Best leave,' Luther told them. When they were gone, Barrett tried reason. 'This is a loco thing you're doing, Rosie. Give me the gun.'

Grimly, Rosie said, 'I swear, Luther Barrett, that if you don't tell me —'

'OK,' Barrett yelped. 'Just stop waving that gun about.' He began, 'You know I love you, Rosie. When you rejected me, I went clean loco . . .'

'And?'

'Well . . . I sent Bellamy looking for Mannion,' he blurted out. Rosie paled. 'Now, I'm really sorry, Rosie. But I can't find Bellamy high or low to call him off.' Distraught, he continued, 'Maybe, once he had my cash in his pocket, Bellamy just took off.'

In a quiet and deadly tone, Rosie said, 'You'll be dead, so help me, if Bellamy kills Dan.' She went forward to place the barrel of the cocked Colt against Luther Barrett's forehead. 'So you'd better pray that you'll find Bellamy, Luther.'

'Hell, you old bastard!' Frank Trump raged against Zachariah, having just discovered the reason for the old man's jitteriness. 'Them 'Paches will skin us 'live!'

'All the more reason we gotta stick t'gether,' Zachariah said, as Frank Trump wheeled his horse in anger, ready to part ways. 'T'gether we've got some chance, Frank. Alone, we ain't got none.'

Frank Trump sneered. 'You old fool. There must be a hundred Indians on our tails. Alone or t'gether ain't goin' to matter none, if they find us.'

Another time Zachariah would have stomped out his son's rebellion. But he was no fool. A man as fired up as Frank Trump was, was as unpredictable as a bushfire fanned by a gale. However, if he saved his hide, he'd remember his son's revolt and lack of respect and punish it. Right now Frank Trump needed feather-light handling, if gunfire was not to be exchanged betwen them. And whatever the outcome of such foolishness, Zachariah figured that he could only be a loser. Either he'd be dead, or alone to face Hunting Wolf and the lawman from Tuteville called Mannion.

'I'm real sorry 'bout the mess I got ya into, son,' Zachariah said silkily. 'But right now we gotta stick t'gether. If'n we don't neither one of us is goin' to come outa this with our skin intact.' His voice was soothing and cajoling, the way a concerned father's might be. 'You gotta right to gun me down here and now, Frank. But I ain't ever claimed to be no saint.' He chuckled. 'And that's a fact you'd be aware of, son.' Holding his breath in check, Zachariah looped an arm around Frank Trump's shoulders, and drew Frank to him. 'If we keep our nerve.' His smile was sly. 'As always, we'll come up Trumps.'

Climbing a rocky precipice, Nathan Trump said, with a leering snigger that heated Dan Mannion's blood beyond the boiling-point that the desert heat had brought it to, 'Be sure you hold on real tight now, Sister. Wouldn't want you fallin' off on that curvy rear end of yours.'

'Shut your filthy mouth, Trump!' the marshal ordered. 'Sister Lucy ain't one of the women you normally cavort with.'

'A woman's a woman, lawman,' the outlaw drawled. 'In my book, created to pleasure a man. Ain't that right, Sister?'

'Keep moving!' Mannion snapped.

Trump asked, 'How far you reckon to Rourke's Trail, Marshal?' Mannion was taken aback. The outlaw sneered. 'Yeah, lawman. If I figured it out, so will my pa and brothers.'

The outlaw rode cockily ahead. He turned in his saddle to whisper in Sister Lucy's ear. On seeing shock freeze the nun's features, Mannion's anger flared. He drew alongside Trump.

'I said shut your filthy mouth, Trump. Or I'll damn well shut it for you!' Mannion tipped his hat to the nun. 'Sorry about the swearing, Sister.'

When the marshal was out of earshot, Nathan Trump proposed to the nun, 'You help me, and I'll return the favour, honey.'

'And if I don't?'

'Oh, but I think, under the circumstances, you surely will.'

Dan Mannion did not know it yet, but the odds of getting Nathan Trump's neck in a noose had begun to stack steeply against him.

# FOURTEEN

The storm finally broke, its downpour bringing relief but also treachery as water flooded down from higher ground, filling every gorge and gully, and creating makeshift rivers which could sweep man and beast away in their swiftly moving waters. Trails vanished under the tides. Dan thanked the Lord that they had reached the rim of the desert country, and were heading into the black-faced hills of Rourke's Trail. He wondered if he should hole up and wait until the storm blew itself out. Seeping residue from the mines would pose a threat, making the trail muddy and uncertain underfoot. But any delay could give the Indians, or the Trumps, the chance to catch up. They were twin evils he wanted to avoid. All things considered, Dan Mannion reckoned that pushing ahead was the safer bet.

They rode on through the storm, Dan accepting

no protest. Rourke's Trail would get greener and more sheltered as they progressed. By the time they reached its midpoint, with its pine-covered slopes, most of the storm's threat would have diminished. There was the risk of falling trees, or trees felled by lightning. But all risks could not be planned for.

'This is loco,' Trump griped, as they faced into the jaws of the storm.

Lightning streaked out of the premature darkness. The air filled with smoke as trees struck by the lightning ignited, and in turn set fire to the undergrowth, forcing them to continually switch to the spider's web of off-shoot trails, all of them holding their own dangers.

Trump was griping again, and Mannion had to admit, with some justification.

'This is like ridin' into Hades, Marshal. This damn mountain is tinder dry. We'll be roasted like pigs on a spit!'

'No point in grousing now,' Mannion observed drily. 'Our backtrail could be worse than what lies ahead.'

'What the hell are ya grinnin' 'bout?' the outlaw challenged the Tuteville lawman.

Mannion said lazily, 'Oh, I've been thinking . . .'

'What 'bout?'

'About your kin, Trump.' He looked at the firestorm building all around them. 'Your pa and

101

brothers might just think that saving your hide isn't worth the risk.'

'Pa would never think that way,' the outlaw barked.

But it pleased Dan Mannion to see the seed of doubt he'd planted grow in Nathan Trump's eyes.

Trump had one last card to play.

'At least think 'bout Sister Lucy, Marshal.'

'I'm really sorry you have to go through this ordeal, Sister,' Dan apologized to the nun. 'But, you see, the way I figure, we've got a choice of evils to decide between. Take our chances with the storm, the Trumps, or the Apaches. Not much of a choice, Sister. I reckon the storm holds less threat than the other options.'

'Talk sense to him,' Trump urged Sister Lucy, in a manner that was downright disrespectful to Dan Mannion's way of thinking.

'Oh, shut up,' Sister Lucy spat, with the fizz of a riled rattler. Conscious of Mannion's gawping stare, her change back to a kindlier tone was instant. 'I'm sure the marshal knows best, Mr Trump.'

'Hope you still think so when one of them lightning rod's fries you, *Sister*,' Trump snarled, emphasizing disparagingly the last word of his statement.

Sister Lucy crossed herself. 'I'll pray that God will see us safely through the storm and all other dangers.'

Nathan Trump scoffed scathingly. 'You think God'll listen to a . . .?' He chewed off the end of the sentence.

An uneasy, sullen truce settled between the nun and the outlaw. Dan wondered about the thorny hostility which had flared. He pondered on Trump's unfinished sentence and his own sudden unease, for which he could not pinpoint the reason. Heading on up Rourke's Trail, Mannion gave over his thoughts to the more pleasant times he hoped were ahead; days and nights spent with Rosie O'Sullivan.

To the rear, Zachariah and Frank Trump were sheltering from the storm at Hannigan's Reach. Not many things scared Zachariah, but lightning was one of them, spiders being a second. Zachariah's dread of lightning was put in his blood when he was three years old and saw his uncle melt when struck by lightning. His fear of spiders was born when his pa had locked him in a cellar full of the crawlers for catawauling about his uncle.

Frank Trump had not inherited his father's phobia about lightning. He did not understand it, and had no sympathy for it. He impatiently paced the trading post, his mood darkening with every passing second.

'We're losin' time,' he complained. 'If we don't move soon, Nathan will be in the Tuteville jail.'

'The storm'll pass soon,' Zachariah snapped irritably.

'That's what you said two hours 'go.' Frank warned, 'Them 'Paches catch us up, and a li'le old streak of lightnin' ain't goin' to seem that important no more, Pa.'

But try as he might there was no prising Zachariah loose from the darkest corner of the post, where he crouched with his hands over his head, cringing at each new explosion of blue-white light.

Frank growled, 'Desert storms can last five minutes or five friggin' hours!'

'Ain't no storm I ever knowed lasted that long,' Zachariah grumbled, crouching deeper into the dark corner as lightning danced about the room.

Frank Trump knew that it was no use mouthing off. There would be no shifting Zachariah until the storm passed. Meanwhile, all he could hope for was that he would not lose his hair, the keeping of which now was his prime concern, and not the rescue of his brother. He paced back and forth to the window, his eyes keenly scanning the storm for any sign of Hunting Wolf and his braves. The first sign, and he'd ride helter-skelter. Pa, and Nathan, too, could go to hell.

Hunting Wolf cursed as the presence of a Cavalry patrol forced a change of direction on him, and a lengthy period of inactivity in a stretch of gullies while the bluecoats put distance between him and them. He also had to deal with the restless young bucks in his party who wanted to take the soldiers' scalps, confident, in their ignorance, of their ability to defeat the horse-soldiers. Hunting Wolf knew better. Though he outnumbered the horse-soldiers, many times he had witnessed the bluecoats' shooting skills and fighting spirit, and he knew that his greenhorn bucks would be no match for them. The plains and desert were filled with the bones of his Apache brothers, evidence of the horse-soldiers' battle-craft. He had seen before the horse-soldiers' chief; whose mane of long yellow hair many an Apache wanted as a trophy, but none had gained.

Hunting Wolf knew, too, that the number of bucks willing to join him each time he raided the white man's farms and ranches grew ever smaller. It would be foolish to lose more in a hopeless cause. Many of the young men had died in the Apache battles to drive the white man from their lands, and of those left, many had lost their courage and had grown weak on the reservations under the influences of the white man.

Many, too, to the shame of their ancestors, had settled for the white man's charity. He could not fight the horse-soldiers as in the old days, when the villages were full of braves and Apache women bore many strong children. Now the women, like their men, consorted with the white man. It pained Hunting Wolf's heart and inflamed his anger against the white-eyes to see his people become nothing more than the white man's slaves; treated no better than mangy dogs. But he would not go to meet the gods whimpering. He would take with him many white-eyes' scalps as an offering. Soon the horse-soldiers would be gone. Then he would ride to the place called Hannigan's Reach, where his scouts had told him the white men he sought were hiding. There he would settle old scores. The white man called Zachariah Trump had made a fool of him; had made him lose face. For that alone he would die. But for the defilement of his sister he would die slowly and very painfully.

Eventually Dan Mannion had to admit that his dogged fight against the ravages and dangers of the storm was one which he could lose at any moment. The last lightning-bolt had sliced a tree in half. It had fallen right across their path, and it was only with luck that its flaming trunk had not crashed down on them. The temptation to push on to Tuteville was difficult to stifle, but if he did so, sheer exhaustion might be the winner, if the storm wasn't. It would be night soon. Sister Lucy was in bad shape, and he wasn't exactly perky himself. Nathan Trump had weathered the storm and the desert best. Yielding, the marshal swung into a cave to wait out the storm.

The cave was deeper than it looked. Around its entrance there was a plentiful supply of bramble and kindling. Mannion got the makings of a fire together, and set it near the mouth of the cave. He collected a couple of spindly branches torn from a nearby tree by the storm. He pointed their ends with his hunting knife, and drove the pointed sticks into the cave's sandy soil. He then hung the blanket from his bedroll on them as a makeshift smoke screen, to prevent the fire's smoke from blowing into the cave and building up inside it. If that happened, in no time at all the cave would fill with smoke and drive them out. Then the accumulated smoke would billow from the cave, and be easily seen by watching eyes. As the fire caught alight Dan was pleased to see that the blanket was a very effective smoke deflector, and that the wind had no difficulty in dispersing the light smoke from the cave entrance. He prepared a meal of beans, coffee, and biscuits.

It both troubled and disappointed the marshal that Sister Lucy had chosen Nathan Trump's company in preference to his. He glanced into the darkness of the cave, and saw Sister Lucy and the outlaw with their heads together, Trump talking in what Dan would call a persuading way. Mannion scowled. What kind of animal was Trump? But then, he thought, what kind of woman was Sister Lucy? To have anything to do with the outlaw.

Sister Lucy, conscious of the marshal's scrutiny, glanced his way. Dan Mannion had no explanation for his sudden unease. The kind of unease a man gets when a snake crawls across his belly.

# FIFTEEN

Luther Barrett rode up through the gap at the end of Rourke's Trail. The storm, which was petering out for Dan Mannion, was only building for Barrett. The wind, howling through the narrow gap, threatened to hoist the rancher from his horse and blow him clear back to the Big B. He had racked his brains trying to figure out where Wes Bellamy had disappeared to, and had come up with the gap, a perfect bushwhacker's lair. It was clever thinking on Bellamy's part. Mannion would have a choice of two approaches to Tuteville, either over Rourke's Trail and through the gap, or across flat open country with little or no cover. In effect it was no choice at all.

Even above the gathering storm, Bellamy, with ears attuned by years of constant vigilance to pick up the slightest sound, heard the scrape of hoof on stone. He quickly doused the lamp, and hurried to the shack window. His narrowed eyes peered into the dusk, and instantly spotted the Big B boss labouring against the wind. He went to the door.

'Howdy, Barrett,' he hailed.

Luther Barrett swung up through the rocks, battered by the wind. He was glad to gain the shack's shelter, dour and dirty as it was.

Bellamy relit the lamp and sprawled on a chair. 'What brings you up here?' he enquired of the rancher. 'Must be pretty urgent to have faced this blower?'

'Change of plans,' Barrett said.

'Yeah?' The gunfigther's eyes glistened with suspicion.

Luther Barrett said, 'I don't want Mannion killed.'

Bellamy snorted. 'What changed your mind?'

'I got to thinking, and it just isn't right.'

Bellamy asked scoffingly, 'You given up on bedding that skirt you've been chasing?'

Barrett fought to control his anger at the gunfighter's mocking and impudent manner.

'No, I haven't. But —'

Bellamy interjected harshly, 'You ain't never going to lift her petticoat while Mannion's still around.'

The rancher's fist shot out and landed squarely on Wes Bellamy's jaw, catapulting him off his chair and back against the shack wall with such force that part of the rotten wall disintegrated under the impact. The gunfighter's anger over-rode his pain. He sprang back on to his feet, his hand diving for iron.

'Hold it!'

Bellamy froze, looking down the barrel of Luther Barrett's Colt. The rancher told him, 'I'll take half my money back. The other half you can use to clear out.'

Bellamy grinned. 'I was kinda looking forward to dispatching the marshal, Barrett.' He massaged his face where the rancher's jaw-buster had landed. 'He punches almost as hard as you do.'

Barrett recalled the gunfighter's brush with the marshal a couple of weeks previously, in which Bellamy had come off the worse for wear. The rancher said, 'I should never have kept you around to begin with, Bellamy.'

The Texan shook his head. 'I'm sure sorry you feel that way, Barrett. But . . .' He shrugged and, took from his pocket the roll of bills which the Big B boss had given him earlier.' 'You sure I can't keep all of this?'

Luther Barrett, relieved that his confrontation with the gunfighter had not turned ugly, did not wrangle further about the money. He conceded. 'Keep the money. Just ride.'

'Now? In this storm?'

'Now!' Barrett barked.

111

Bellamy drawled, 'A mite unfriendly, neighbour.'

The rancher's stance was uncompromising. 'That's the deal, Bellamy. Take it or leave it.'

'And if I don't take it?' the gunfighter asked with quiet menace.

'Well, then, I've got a decision to make.'

'Which would be?'

Cold-eyed, Luther Barrett stated, 'Kill you. Or take you back to town.' He snorted. 'Now, seeing that I wouldn't want you to get the drop on me heading back to town . . .'

Wes Bellamy laughed. He pocketed the money, grabbed his hat from the table, smoothed his hair down, and placed the Stetson on his head at an angle that had often had the rancher wondering how it stayed on. 'Mind if I have a smoke before I go?'

'Guess not,' Barrett said. 'But make it fast. I don't want to be blown clear to Mexico by this storm.'

The gunfighter quickly rolled a smoke. Then he bent down to light the quirly from the lamp's bowl.

His movement was casual and unthreatening, up to the second he grabbed the lamp and flung it at the rancher. The lamp struck Luther Barrett on the chest. Its oil spilled out and ignited. A *whoosh* of flame threatened the rancher's face. He staggered back beating at the flames. Only a split second had passed, but it was enough time for Wes Bellamy's gun to clear leather and spit. Luther Barrett doubled up, holding his gut, his eyes pleading. His plea got no mercy from the gunfighter. The Texan's next bullet went right between the rancher's eyes. Bellamy stamped out the fire on the shack floor. Then he searched Barrett and relieved him of what money he had, along with his gold pocket-watch. He dragged the rancher's body to the shack door and tossed it into the rocks. Calmly, he rolled another smoke. He counted the takings from his robbery, which amounted to 150 dollars. Smiling, he added this to his bundle, observing wryly:

'Why, Mr Bellamy, sir. You're fast becoming a man of substance.'

# SIXTEEN

Nathan Trump told the woman masquerading as Sister Lucy, but known to him as Lady Lil, a cantina singer, 'Way I see it, you ain't got no choice but do as I tell ya, honey.'

Lady Lil replied, but with no great confidence in her ability to challenge Trump: 'I could walk right up to the marshal and tell him you want me to kill him.'

'Yeah?' Trump growled, his smile wolfish. 'He's a lawman, gal. Straight as they come. Sure as night follows day, Mannion will ship you back 'cross the border to be strung up for murder.'

'Why should they hang me?' Lady Lil argued. 'It wasn't murder. You can't murder an animal, and that's what Captain Miguel Suárez was. He tried to rape me.'

Trump scoffed. 'If you ain't 'fraid they'll string ya, Lil, how come you're runnin' like a scared jack-rabbit?' His eyes locked with the cantina singer's.

' 'Cause you know the Mex soldiery don't take kindly to women who keep their legs closed to their officers.' His voice dropped to a hoarse whisper. 'Particularly to officers like Suárez, whose uppity family would have the skin off their backs if they showed any inkling of compassion to a whore.'

'I'm not a whore,' Lady Lil grated. 'All I do is sing.'

Nathan Trump shrugged. 'Same thing to grandees like the Suárez.' The outlaw sniggered evilly. 'You're right, Lil. They won't hang you. Them Mex soldier boys'll just tie you 'tween a coupla wagons goin' in diff'rent directions.' He snorted. 'After they've had their fun, that is.' Trump's hand grabbed her arm and squeezed it until its flesh flattened against bone. 'All you gotta do is smash Mannion's skull when he ain't lookin'. That way, you and me ain't goin' to see the devil face to face for a spell yet.' He smiled with coaxing charm. 'Who knows, we might even travel together for a spell, Lil.'

Dan Mannion wished he knew what Trump was saying to the nun. What could he possibly have to say that would grab her attention the way he had? What could Sister Lucy have in common with a man of Trump's ilk? Maybe, Dan speculated, she was trying to convert him, as it was a duty of her calling to try. This speculation brought a wry smile to the Tuteville marshal's lips. Nathan Trump's soul was already bought and paid for by Satan. Whatever the gist of their conversation, it was clear that the outlaw had the upper hand. Mannion reckoned that he'd have to be careful. A nun Sister Lucy might be, but Nathan Trump had a charmer's way about him when he needed to. If the woman in Sister Lucy took over from the nun in Sister Lucy . . . .

'Shit!' Frank Trump swore, when two curious Apaches took to watching Hannigan's Reach. A couple of minutes later his breath caught in his throat when two became four. 'You old fool,' he berated Zachariah. 'Due to your cringin', we'll be lucky if we hold on to our hair. Never saw a grown man whimper the way you do when lightnin's 'bout.'

The storm was moving away to the east, but it was a slow mover and would not clear for maybe an hour yet. Its lightning-bolts were less frequent now, but Zachariah Trump still cowered in the darkest corner of the trading post.

'We gotta ride, Pa,' Frank Trump urged him. 'Afore any more of them murderin' bastards gather.' Glancing through the window, Zachariah Trump's eyes bleached white with fear as a flash dazzled him, and he cowered again. 'You wanna die in this stinkin' shithole?' Frank raged.

'Soon,' Zachariah mumbled.

'Soon ain't good 'nuff,' Frank snarled back, contemptuous and totally uncomprehending of his father's fear. How could a man who had often ridden through hell be turned to jelly by lightning and little bitty spiders? Made no sense at all. 'We'd have caught up with that lawman by now, if you hadn't spent the last coupla hours or more in that damn corner.'

Frank Trump blanched on seeing another three Indians.

'Seven damn 'Paches now,' he panicked. 'You comin' outa that corner or not, Pa? I ain't hangin' round here 'nother minute.'

Encouraged by the fact that there had not been a flash of lightning for a good five minutes, Zachariah crept from his corner on all fours, keeping as close to the floor as his belly would allow. 'They ain't goin' to 'tack 'til that bloodthirsty son-of-a-sow Hunting Wolf gets here,' he promised Frank.

'And that could be any second now,' Frank tossed back. Unconsciously his fingers played with the mane of red hair that fell below his shirt collar. 'I figger we better slip out the back way, and bolt for Rourke's Trail, Pa. That's surely the route the Tuteville marshal will take to deliver Nathan to the hangman.'

Zachariah and Frank Trump shared a common problem with Dan Mannion.

'Bolt? How long d'ya think our nags will hold out before foldin'?'

'What d'ya suggest,' Frank fumed. 'Sit here and lose our scalps?' Frank Trump cleverly played on his father's fears. 'I figger I'll die quick. I reckon it won't be the same for you, Pa.'

Zachariah's fear of what Hunting Wolf had in mind for him overcame his terror of the waning storm. Even now that the storm was almost spent, his skin crawled at the prospect of being in open country while there was the slightest chance of further lightning. Sometimes, too, storms curled back on themselves. However, facing Hunting Wolf instilled an even greater dread in him. For Zachariah, it was a toss-up between probable death in the storm, and a certain and lingering death at the hands of the Indian. At least, he consoled himself, lightning would be mercifully quick compared to any death that Hunting Wolf would dream up for him. Zachariah had seen men die at the hands of the Apache, and it had made even his cruel nature squirm.

'Guess we don't have a choice, Frank,' Zachariah concluded. 'Best try and outrun those redskin bastards, if we can.'

Gallishly, Frank complained, 'You should've told me and Jed the full story 'bout why you and that ren'gade Huntin' Wolf ain't none too friendly,

118

Pa, afore we rode into this hell's nest of vipers. Ain't fair to keep that kinda info'mation from a body, Pa.'

Zachariah Trump was chilled by the angry fire glowing in his son's eyes.

Frank Trump said frostily, 'Needs settlin' 'tween you and me when this shindig's over, Pa.'

'Sure, boy,' Zachariah placated, and instantly made plans to have any settlement go his way. With Jed dead, and Nathan as good as, Zachariah reckoned the Trump gang had ridden its last trail anyway. There was a fat whore in Mexico, as ugly as mortal sin, but full of tricks that lured men to her like moths to a flame. That's where he was headed. Conchita would make good money, and pleasure him when he had a hankering for pleasure. A man could do a whole lot worse, he figured.

As they galloped away from Hannigan's Reach, two Indians paced them.

'Chartin' our trail, I guess,' Zachariah opined. 'Leavin' sign for Huntin' Wolf to follow.'

Ten miles south of Hannigan's Reach, Captain Daniel Thompson, a veteran of a hundred battles with the Apache, and the one whose tactical skills and fighting spirit Hunting Wolf feared, was receiving a report from his scout that pinpointed the whereabouts of the raiding Apaches. Thompson questioned his scout's report.

'Rourke's Trail, you say?'

'That's where they're headed, Captain,' the scout confirmed.

'Wrong direction.' Thompson pointed south. 'Mexico is that way.'

'My bet, sir,' the scout said, 'is that Hunting Wolf is chasing Zachariah Trump. He's also heading for Rourke's Trail.'

'Zachariah Trump? Why would Hunting Wolf be chasing him? It's a well-known fact that Trump and the Apaches are almost kin.'

'You've had a spell in Washington, Captain. While you've been gone, seems Zachariah's been up to some tricks which've raised Hunting Wolf's hackles.' The scout relayed the story he'd heard about the dud rifles which Zachariah Trump had passed off on Hunting Wolf.

Thompson said, 'Well, I guess that would be reason enough for Hunting Wolf wanting to get his hands on Trump.'

Acting on his scout's advice, Thompson ordered his troop to a quick canter. The cavalry captain, having expected Hunting Wolf to be heading for the mountain trails back to Mexico by now, had ground to make up.

The woman known as Lady Lil in the cantinas of the Mexican border towns that were havens for riff-raff like the Trumps, cursed her luck to have crossed paths with Nathan Trump. She had, as her mother would have said, jumped from the frying-pan into the fire.

Mother Francis, the leader of the small group of nuns, had allowed Lil to masquerade as a nun to escape the wrath of Miguel Suárez's comrades. The reverend mother had nursed Lil after the terrible beating Suárez had inflicted on her, putting antiseptic and ointment on the many cigarette burns on her breasts and stomach. But fate had been cruel to her, delivering her back into the hands of a man like Trump, and she was now faced with the most awful dilemma. Lil struggled with her conscience. If she told Dan Mannion about Trump's treachery she'd save his hide, but sink herself. Chances were that, being a lawman, the Tuteville marshal would incarcerate her along with Trump, until she was handed back to the Mexican authorities. Not long ago, the killer of a Mexican need have no fear of such a thing happening. But times were changing. Treaties were being signed, and Mexico was being seen as a neighbour rather than the enemy she once was. Trump summed up perfectly the bind she was in.

'Ain't no use worryin' your pretty head, Lil. Don't see that you've much choice but to help me, if you wanna help yourself. So what ya waitin' for?' the outlaw demanded.

'The right time of course,' Lil answered grumpily.

'Seems to me that any time's the right time, with what you've gotta offer a man, Lil.'

'Maybe as you see it,' she said. 'But a nun getting all man-friendly is kind of off-putting to a decent man.'

Nathan Trump shrugged. 'A man's a man, Lil.'

Lil said, 'We need a plan.'

'What kinda plan?'

She leaned close to him to explain in a whisper, hating every second of her treachery. Lil's whispering brought a broad smile to Nathan Trump's face. The outlaw massaged his jaw. 'If you're goin' to slap my face, make it look like you mean it, honey.'

'I will mean it,' she said.

Alerted by the slap to Nathan Trump's face that had the crack of a rifle shot in the confines of the cave, Mannion spun round. He saw, as was planned, Sister Lucy struggling to fight off Nathan Trump's advances. Incensed by the outrage, the marshal's instincts kicked in. If he had taken a second to think, he would have realized that with his hands cuffed, Trump's assault could only be a token one, easily fought off. Mannion strode to the rear of the cave and yanked Trump's head back by his greasy hair. Sister Lucy wiped her mouth and spat out the foul taste of his lips.

'I should kill you right here and now,' the marshal raged at the outlaw.

The lawman's anger made him blind to Lady Lil slipping behind him. Dan Mannion's surprise was total when he felt the Colt .45 slide from his holster and prod his spine.

'Don't move a muscle, Marshal,' Lil said.

Nathan Trump sprang to his feet. 'That was a real good plan, Lil. Get the keys to the cuffs.'

'I'm sorry, Marshal,' Lil apologized, unlocking the outlaw's handcuffs. 'But I didn't have a choice.'

Mannion was puzzled. 'You're a nun, for God's sake.'

Free of the handcuffs, Nathan Trump massaged his wrists to ease their cramp. His grin spread from ear to ear. 'Nun?' He looped an arm around Lady Lil's waist and lewdly pressed her against him, his hands roaming freely. 'Marshal,' he announced, 'this here is Lady Lil. And she's as far away from a nun as you can get. In fact she's a cantina whore —'

'Singer,' Lady Lil interjected hotly.

Trump sniggerd. 'Sure, honey.' He continued his explanation for Mannion's benefit. 'Lady Lil is wanted for the murder of a fella by the name of Miguel Suárez. That would be Cap'ain Suárez, Marshal.' Mannion had had many surprises in his life, but this one knocked him for six.

Trump grabbed Mannion's Colt from Lil's shaking hand. 'Better let me have that afore there's a' awful accident, honey.'

In the split second before Trump grabbed the gun from her, Lady Lil had been tempted to shoot the outlaw and take her chances with Dan Mannion. But her hesitation lost her the opportunity to right the wrong she'd done the marshal.

'Thought for a spell there, Lil,' Trump drawled, his eyes hooded, 'that you were goin' to drill me. Now that would be a mighty unfriendly thing to do.'

He grabbed Lil by the hair and kissed her fully on the mouth, gyrating against her. Then he shoved her towards the cave entrance. 'Time to ride.'

Lil looked anxiously from Mannion to Trump. 'You don't have to kill the marshal, Nathan.'

'No, I don't,' the outlaw agreed. 'I wan' to. 'Sides we don't wan' our trail dogged by no lawman, Lil.'

Lil said desperately, 'He won't track us. Will you, Marshal?'

'To hell and back,' Mannion flung back.

'See,' Trump gloated. 'What'd I tell ya.'

'Clever ploy,' Mannion told Lady Lil, indicating the nun's habit. 'Mexico, being a Catholic country, I don't imagine you had much difficulty in crossing the border.'

'This,' Lil fluffed up the habit's skirts, 'was not

my idea. Mother Francis, the reverend mother, thought up the idea.'

Dan was sceptical. 'A nun. Hiding a killer?'

'I'm no killer, mister!' Lil flared. 'The pig I killed deserved killing!'

'That isn't the way Mex law will reckon it,' Dan replied.

Lady Lil shrugged. 'Can't do much about that now, can I.'

Trump sneered. 'Ain't that the truth, Lil. But, true, that Cap'ain Suárez was a real bad apple, Marshal. Liked to burn gals with them stinkin' cheroots he smoked.'

'That true?' Dan questioned Lady Lil.

Lil hung her head low to avoid Mannion's searching gaze. 'It's true,' she murmured.

'Then why did you run?' Dan quizzed. 'Seems to me that a man who does that kind of thing to a woman deserves what he gets.'

Lady Lil scoffed. 'Bless your goodness, Marshal Mannion. But I don't have your kind of faith. I'm a saloon singer. Suárez came from a long line of blue-bloods. His family owns land as far as the eye can see. His uncle is an adviser to the President.' She locked defiant eyes with Mannion. 'Now, Marshal. What chance do you think I had of avoiding a rope, or worse?'

Mannion said, 'If you're telling the truth, your body bore the evidence of Suárez's cruelty,'

'Like I said, I'm a saloon singer, and that to most folk means whore. It'd be easy for Suárez to claim that it was someone else's doing. Suárez would have simply picked out another man and hanged him to cover himself.'

By now, moved to compassion by Lady Lil's sad story, Dan Mannion's anger was mollified. 'What were you doing in Mexico to begin with?' he enquired in a kindly tone.

'I had a loco husband, who thought that sod-busting in Mexico would be better than turning the soil on the American side of the Rio Grande. When his first crop came in, the local military commander reckoned that he should take half the profits of Luke's work. My man figured differently, and earned himself a bullet in the back. The land and crop was confiscated. That left me with a choice to make: be the commander's exclusive whore, or be a cantina singer. I chose the cantina.'

Dan knew that her story was not uncommon. A lot of women in the cathouses of the West and Mexico were women who had lost their men for one reason or another, and had been left with only one asset to cash in on.

Nathan Trump snorted. 'Don't you two go gettin' cosy now.'

'What's your real name?' Mannion asked the woman.

126

'Lillian Brennan.'

'Well, Lillian Brennan,' the Tuteville marshal drawled. 'Don't you go trusting this one.' His eyes swivelled towards Trump. 'You're staying right here with me.'

For a moment, hope shone in Lil's eyes; hope that quickly faded.

'I wish I'd met a man like you a long time ago, Marshal.'

Mannion smiled. 'Sorry, Lillian. I'm spoken for.' He added, his smile wry, 'I hope.'

Lillian said, 'I've got to take my chances with Trump, Marshal. If you're as iron-backed a lawman as Nathan says, you'd send me back across the Rio to a rope. A damn noose I don't deserve.'

'Maybe,' Dan conceded. 'Then maybe not. Seems to me that you had good reason to dispatch this Suárez *hombre*.' His gaze held Lillian Brennan's. 'Your tale surely gives me food for thought, Lillian.'

Trump snarled, 'Now, Lil. Don't you let the marshal put no fancy notions in your head, gal. He's a lawman, and you're wanted for murder. Leopards don't change their spots.'

'He's right,' Lillian said.

'You bet I am, Lil,' Trump intoned. His flying boot caught Mannion in the belly. 'That should shut your mouth, Marshal,' he screamed.

'There was no call to do that,' Lillian said, helping Dan straighten up.

Trump cocked the Colt he held. 'We've wasted 'nuff time.'

Dan Mannion could see the swirl of indecision and confusion that was Lillian Brennan's lot. 'Suárez might have deserved to die, Lillian,' the Tuteville marshal said. 'But killing me will be cold-blooded murder. American law will hunt you down. And you can't hightail it back to Mexico.'

'No one has called me Lillian in a long time,' she said, her eyes dewy.

Nathan Trump drew a bead on Mannion. 'Say hi-do to the devil for me, Marshal.'

Lillian Brennan sprang to Dan Mannion's defence, standing in front of him. 'We can just ride away from here, Nathan,' she said. 'There's no call to kill the marshal.'

'Like I said, I'm goin' to enjoy it.' He growled, 'Now step aside, Lil.'

'No,' she said adamantly.

'Damn it, Lil,' the outlaw swore. 'Don't make me have to drill through ya. 'Cause I will if I have to.'

Mannion fumed at his helplessness to do anything about his coming demise. His thoughts were of Rosie O'Sullivan. He had only one comfort, and that was that Luther Barrett, who was also in love with Rosie, would look after her –

not that she needed looking after.

'Step aside, Lil,' Trump raged.

'No!'

'Well, then, it's your funeral.'

Dan Mannion's life was counting down in seconds. Nathan Trump's finger, coiled around the Colt's trigger, was tightening. Any second now the explosion that would send him plunging into eternity would come.

'I'm not going to let you kill the marshal in cold blood,' Lillian Brennan warned Trump.

Trump barked, 'Didn't seem to trouble ya none while back.'

'Since then I've got sense,' Lillian spat. 'I should never have listened to you.'

'Don't throw away your life, Lillian,' Dan pleaded. 'He'll do as he says.'

Lillian Brennan stood her ground, eyes flashing in defiance. Mannion shoved her aside, and stood squarely facing Trump. The outlaw instantly stepped back, opening up a sizeable gap between him and Mannion to counter any lunge by the lawman. Lillian, nearer to Trump, sprang at him, her nails clawing his face. He howled. Mannion grabbed his chance and leaped through the air at the outlaw. Trump's hastily delivered shot buzzed off the wall behind Dan. It snarled round the cave looking for a target, and almost found one in Lillian as it whined past her right

ear. In the murky confines of the cave, the flash
from the gun momentarily unsighted the
marshal. Lillian, to the side of the outlaw, was
not as affected by the Colt's flash, and she took
advanatge of Trump's concentration in dealing
with Mannion to throw a rock at his head. It fell
short, but collided with Trump's right shoulder,
the solid impact eliciting a howl of pain from the
outlaw, a pain which shot down his arm to his
fingers, forcing him to drop the six-gun. Mannion,
lightning-quick to grab his chance, swung a boot
that caught Trump on the kneecap. The outlaw's
left leg buckled under him. Off balance, Trump
hobbled backwards. Showing no mercy, Mannion
followed through with a series of blows that had
the outlaw reeling and desperately trying to
counter the marshal's blistering onslaught.
Mannion easily parried Trump's feeble attempts
at a comeback, and landed several gut-crippling
fists in the outlaw's midriff. In a vicious change of
direction, the outlaw side-swiped Lillian, rattling
her brain in its cranium. She was catapulted
back by Trump's blow, and crashed heavily
against the wall. She dropped unconscious to the
floor.

Concern for Lillian Brennan diverted
Mannion's attention from the task in hand.
Trump grabbed his chance and landed a jaw-
buster on the left side of the lawman's face that

scattered his eyesight and his wits. The walls of the cave closed in on Dan Mannion. He fought desperately to sidestep the outlaw's second launched fist aimed at making contact with his right jaw. A fortunate stagger on the rock-strewn floor, more than any planned avoidance tactic on the marshal's part, sent him askew, and Trump's pile-driver glided harmlessly past.

A victim of his own powerful lunge to put every ounce of spite into his hammer-blow, Nathan Trump went tumbling awkwardly past the Tuteville lawman. Dan Mannion helped him on his way with a mulekick blow to the back of the outlaw's head, which increased Trump's hapless momentum. When he crashed against the cave's end wall he was at his most helpless, and took the full brunt of the collision.

Mannion put the handcuffs back on Nathan Trump, and, not needing to worry about the outlaw for the immediate future, gently nursed Lillian Brennan back to consciousness. However, his problems were not over. As he rolled a smoke, rifle fire peppered the mouth of the cave, forcing Mannion and Lillian back into the cave's deepest recess.

'Lawman. Tuteville lawman,' Zachariah Trump hailed. 'You hand over my boy, and we'll go our sep'rate ways.'

Dan sighed heavily. Nathan Trump's kin had

caught him up, and it looked like they held all the aces in the deck.

# SEVENTEEN

Dan Mannion could only hold out in the cave for a short spell. The rock-strewn terrain offered plenty of cover for a patient man to converge on the cave with little risk to himself. Or the Trumps could simply sit tight and wait. However, whichever way they played it, Mannion knew that he was in deep trouble. Another problem was that the longer the siege lasted, the greater the risk of Indian trouble, too. The marshal had no way of knowing that the arrival of the Apaches was the last thing the Trumps wanted. He had heard of Zachariah's trading with the Indians, and was reckoning on them being a help rather than a threat to the outlaws. Mannion's anger was directed at himself for not having weathered the storm and put distance between himself and his pursuers. The high country, with its generous tree-cover and look-out points over his back trail would have given him a clear edge, which he'd squandered. He had been foolish to draw rein when minutes counted. Now he could pay with his life for that error of judgement.

Nathan Trump was his old cocky self, predicting, 'My pa will skin you 'live, lawman.'

The marshal did not doubt the truth of the outlaw's prediction. He crept to the edge of the cave entrance, but was careful to remain within its shadows, to try and spot the shooters. He saw Zachariah and Frank Trump crouched behind boulders, high up, either side of the cave. They were ideally located to deliver a murderous cross-fire, should he try and break from the cave. He could not shoot in two directions at once, and, if he tried to choose alternate targets, at any given time he'd be wide open to the Trumps' second gun. And where was Jed Trump? Maybe he was dead? Or maybe he'd lit out for safer territory? He could also be the nasty surprise in the woodpile. Another problem was . . .

Mannion's gaze settled on the Winchester in his saddle scabbard, where he had foolishly left it, anxious as he had been to get Sister Lucy, as he had thought of her then, in out of the storm. Without a rifle, his chances, which were slim at best, were reduced to nil. To get hold of the Winchester, he would have to cover about a hundred feet to his horse, across open ground. Normally, a hundred feet was not a lot of ground.

But under a blistering crossfire, delivered by gun-handy *hombres* like Zachariah and Frank Trump, he figured it was probably ninety-nine feet too much.

Mannion had Lillian Brennan to worry about, too. He knew that for a woman to fall into the Trumps' clutches was pretty much the same as falling into Apache hands.

'The Trumps?' Lillian asked, fretfully.

'The Trumps,' Mannion confirmed.

'What're you going to do, Marshal?'

'Try and get hold of that rifle, I guess.'

Concern flashed in Lillian Brennan's blue eyes. 'They'd cut you to ribbons.'

'Likely,' the Tuteville marshal admitted. 'But they hold all the aces, Lillian. They can sit and wait. Creep up on us. Or wait for their Apache friends to show up.' Mannion took shells from his gunbelt and replenished the empty chambers of his .45. He handed the pistol to Lillian. 'Cover me as best you can.'

'I've never fired a gun in my life,' she wailed.

'Doesn't make any difference. Might as well be slinging pebbles.' He chuckled. 'But the noise might help.'

'What about him?' she asked fearfully, her eyes flashing Nathan Trump's way.

Dan Mannion said resolutely, 'If he moves, kill him.' He crouched low. 'Ready?'

Lillian Brennan said, 'As I'll ever be.'

Dan grimaced at the pain in his leg, inflicted during his skirmish with the Apaches. The muscles and sinews throbbed and burned. He could only pray that the leg would not buckle under him. If that happened, he was a deadman.

Lillian Brennan said softly, 'Good luck, Dan.'

In that moment, seeing the true woman inside the cantina singer known as Lady Lil, Dan Mannion made a decision which, with luck, he'd be able to act on. He said, 'The second I move, you start shooting.'

'I will,' she promised.

'I'm counting on you, Lillian Brennan.'

Lillian smiled a sad smile. 'No one's done that in a long time, Dan Mannion.'

Sending a final surge of adrenaline into his legs, the marshal broke from the cave to be instantly caught in a deadly crossfire. As he sprinted, forcing his injured leg to keep going when it wanted to give up, bullets buzzed around him. He had not gone far when he believed in miracles. Because there was no way, other than by divine intervention, that he should still be standing. Trump bullets spat grit in his face, while jagged slivers of rock spun around him. A couple of the needle-sharp missiles bit and nicked him, but, blessedly, so far, had not caused him serious injury. He was only feet from his horse, and that precious Winchester.

Added to the marshal's problems was Lillian Brennan's wild shooting. The bullets coming from the cave were every bit as likely to down him as were the Trumps. The outlaws were finding Mannion's range, and beginning to judge more accurately his weaving sprint. Mannion knew that it could only be seconds now before he was blasted, either by the Trumps' design, or Lillian Brennan's mistake.

# EIGHTEEN

'Plug the lawman, ya stupid bitch!' Nathan Trump screamed at Lillian, conscious of Mannion having the kind of luck that might just end in him swinging from a rope. Instead, Lillian fired in Nathan Trump's direction. The bullet took a chunk from the rock inches above his head. He dived to the ground, whining, 'You gone loco, Lil?'

'Be sure you keep your face in the dirt,' Lillian warned. 'I'd soon kill you as hear another word pass your lips.'

Nathan Trump swallowed hard. He believed her.

The Tuteville marshal had his hand on the Winchester's walnut grip and was pulling it clear of its scabbard. He could not believe that he'd made it this far. He dropped to the ground as a bullet cut a furrow across his saddle, and returned fire into the rocks. Flashes flew off the boulder behind which Zachariah Trump had taken cover, forcing him to duck. Taking advantage of the Trump patriarch's absence, Mannion sprinted into the rocks directly below Zachariah, and quickly worked his way upwards. He had gained an important advantage. The boulder behind which Zachariah was hiding, bulged out over the rocky track. Zachariah's shooting angle had become more acute, and became sharper still the further along the track Mannion progressed. For Zachariah to get a clear shot at him, he had to risk more and more exposure to the marshal's rifle.

Frank Trump, too, had become disadvantaged, as Mannion craftily used the boulder-strewn track to dodge from cover to cover in short runs, exposing himself only fleetingly to Frank Trump's fire. Any chance of nailing the lawman was fading fast, without taking the kind of risk which Frank Trump was increasingly not of a mind to take.

Frank saw that, fortunately for him, the Tuteville lawman had made nailing Zachariah his first priority. Frank Trump glanced to the cave. With the marshal concentrating on sending Zachariah to hell, he had a chance to rescue Nathan. The woman was clearly an amateur with a shooting-iron, and would pose no great risk to his hide. However, if he hung around to rescue Nathan, he would probably, by then, have to face the marshal, whose grit was not in short supply.

Such a prospect was not one which Frank Trump anticipated with relish. So much gunfire would bring all sorts of trouble. Apache and Army. The Indians would skin him, and the army would hand him over for hanging, if they bothered in the first place. Maybe now was the time to strike out on his own, and to hell with Zachariah and Nathan.

'Frank!' Zachariah Trump's holler echoed through the rocks. 'You still suckin' air?'

'Yeah, Pa. I'm still suckin'.'

'Then get shootin', boy.'

'Sure, Pa,' Frank called back, and cut loose with a token volley. He had made up his mind to abandon Zachariah to the marshal's rifle, and Nathan to the Tuteville lawman's rope.

Lillian Brennan gasped and her heart almost thundered to a halt, as she saw Dan Mannion take a tumble on the end of Frank Trump's shot.

'Got him, Pa,' Frank Trump called out exultantly, and added, 'Heh, Nathan, the lawman's down.'

Nathan Trump sneered. 'Guess you backed the wrong man, Lady Lil.'

'Don't call me that!' Lillian grated.

'I'll damn well call you whatever,' Trump snarled. His face reflected his licentious thoughts. 'I'm goin' to enjoy you, Lil'

Lillian Brennan knew she should sink lead in

140

him right then and there, but her conscience would not allow her to kill even a hogward like Nathan Trump in cold blood. But . . . She settled the Colt .45 squarely on Nathan Trump. 'On your feet,' she ordered. Trump stood up. 'Go to the mouth of the cave.'

At the cave entrance, Lillian put the barrel of the Colt to the outlaw's head. She grittily warned Zachariah Trump, 'If the marshal is alive, and you harm a hair on his head, I'll cut your son down.' She called out. 'Can you hear me, Dan?'

Lying still in the rocks, Mannion cursed silently. Events had taken an unexpected turn. His tumble, coming on the end of Frank Trump's shot had been a clever ruse, to give the impression to the Trumps that Frank's shot had counted. Now his trickery had horribly backfired.

Lillian called again, desperation in her voice, 'Talk to me, Dan.'

Reluctantly, Dan Mannion replied, 'I'm alive, Lillian.' His ruse had been wasted, but he had a deep respect for Lillian Brennan's fortitude. But had his trickery been completely wasted? Maybe not. 'Alive, but badly busted up, Lillian,' he added, putting pain in his response.

'You hear that, Pa?' Frank Trump delightedly called out.

'I heard,' Zachariah Trump called back. Then, 'The woman in the cave, you hearing me?'

141

'I hear you,' Lillian called back.

'This is the deal,' the Trump patriarch said. 'You show yourself, and let my boy walk free. And I'll let you and the lawman be.'

'Don't listen to him, Lillian,' Dan Mannion pleaded. 'I can't be of any help to you. He'll cut you down the second you show your face.'

'You show, ma'am,' Zachariah said. 'Or I'll ramble down through these rocks and finish off the lawman.'

'You do that, and I'll kill Nathan,' Lillian cautioned.

Zachariah chuckled. 'I figger you ain't got the grit to kill Nathan in cold blood, ma'am. I also figger that you don't want the marshal's blood on your hands. All in all, I reckon you've got to trust me.'

'Don't listen to him, Lillian,' Mannion warned. 'He'll kill us both.'

Dan Mannion's grey eyes sparked joyously as, cocky as a satisfied rooster, Zachariah Trump stood on the boulder behind which he was hiding, making a perfect target. Zachariah raised his rifle and aimed it at Mannion, lying helplessly, as he thought, on the track below him.

'I've got the lawman in my sights, ma'am,' the outlaw said. 'What's it to be?'

'Good question, Trump,' Mannion said, springing to his feet, rifle spitting from the hip.

Zachariah Trump died carrying a look of

surprise into hell as Mannion put two bullets in his heart, an inch apart. He toppled headlong from the boulder. The rocks were filled with the gut-churning snap of breaking bones.

Frank Trump, stunned by the suddeness of the switch in fortunes, delayed for a vital second; a second which Dan Mannion gladly grabbed. The marshal's rifle spat again, and the single bullet blasted the left side of the outlaw's head away.

'Pa,' Nathan Trump wailed, and getting no response his wail reached a new pitch, 'Frank . . .'

Lillian Brennan said, not unsympathetically, even though she had had her fill a long time ago of men like Nathan Trump. 'You're calling up the dead, Nathan.'

The outlaw staggered about the cave, his eyes wild with the vision of the hangman's rope which he now certainly faced. The woman known as Lady Lil in the cantinas of Mexico understood Trump's fear; it was a fear shared. If Dan Mannion acted as a lawman should act, her date with the hangman, or worse, was not far away either. Sensing Lillian Brennan's trepidation, Nathan Trump played his last card.

'Lil,' he said, 'we're both doomed. Any second now the marshal will be walkin' back in here, unsuspectin', 'cause he's figurin' on you as a friend . . .'

Lillian Brennan felt the presence of the Devil

at her shoulder. 'You've got a gun, Lil,' Trump whispered feverishly. 'Use it, and we'll both cheat the hangman.'

A cold sweat was driven through Lillian's pores by the heat of the temptation coursing through her.

Trump said, 'Mannion is a lawman first and foremost. He'll ship you back to Mexico for sure, Lil.' The sound of Mannion approaching took Lillian Brennan's fever of temptation to a new pitch. 'It's our last chance, Lil,' Trump urged. 'Use the damn gun!'

Time was running out. Dan Mannion's shadow had entered the cave ahead of him. A couple of seconds and he'd follow.

'Kill him, Lil!' Nathan Trump screamed when the marshal appeared. Lillian Brennan swung about to face the Tuteville marshal, awash with indecision. She cocked the six-gun. 'Go on, Lil,' Trump urged her. 'Plug him!'

Mannion said calmly, 'You're not a killer, Lillian.'

He walked towards her, measuring his steps. Lillian Brennan was at a crossroads, with her emotions spinning like a feather in a storm. Fear could make her pull the trigger. It was a gamble, coming at the tail end of a host of gambles. How long could his luck hold for?

Mannion believed in his heart that Lillian

Brennan was not a killer. He had already decided not to ship her back to Mexico, where he knew justice to be in short supply, and corruption flourished. He believed that Lillian, in killing Suárez, had acted in self-preservation. A right, he believed, any woman faced with the horror of rape and torture had.

The next couple of seconds would prove his assessment of Lillian Brennan's character to be right or wrong. If he had perspiration left in him, Mannion would sweat. He was tempted to tell Lillian of his decision not to send her back to Mexico, but he stifled the urge. She had to make a free decision to hand over the Colt to prove to him, beyond all doubt, that she was not a killer. He held out his hand for the six-gun. A fraught second passed before Lillian Brennan handed over the .45 and collapsed weakly into Dan Mannion's arms.

'Trump,' the marshal said grim-faced, 'you've got a date with the Tuteville hangman. You, fella, are a hangman's lot!'

# NINETEEN

Crisis done and dusted, Mannion said, 'Best we move on now.'

'Move on,' Trump cried in desperation. Every step from now on took him nearer a noose. 'It's a'most night.'

Glancing at the shadow-filled sky left in the wake of the storm, the marshal said, 'There's an hour, maybe a little more of light left.'

'This trail is more dangerous than a rattler's spit, Mannion,' the outlaw rightly pointed out. 'Put a foot wrong, and you could fall off this damn mountain.'

Trump had stated the case correctly, but Dan Mannion had three reasons for risking the trail; having flouted death twice he did not want to do so again. There were, he suspected, Indians on the prowl. There was no evidence of their presence, but then there never was until they appeared as if by magic. The army might have them on the run,

146

and he could hope that they had, but waiting around would be a gamble, and he'd had more than enough gambling for this outing. The third reason he wanted to make tracks was the most important of all. He wanted to see Rosie O'Sullivan with a desperation that almost unhinged his sanity.

Mannion said, 'The gunfire will bring Indians swarming like flies around filth.'

'By now the 'Paches are haring back to Mexico with their tails 'tween their pagan legs,' Trump argued.

'That may be so,' the Tuteville marshal conceded in a quiet tone. 'But what if they're not?'

Lillian Brennan shivered. 'I'd prefer a rope to an Apache any day.'

'It's settled,' Mannion growled when the outlaw tried to continue his protest.

Though Nathan Trump had argued that the army had probably put the run on Hunting Wolf and his scalp-hunting renegades, his secret wish was that they had not. The Apaches had earlier acted mighty unfriendly towards him, he being a Trump. However, the Apaches were now his only hope of salvation from a rope. Slim, though that hope was, it was the only hope on offer.

Mannion found Zachariah and Frank Trump's horses in a nearby canyon and took them in tow. Like their own mounts, the outlaws' horses were in poor shape, but by riding all the horses for short spells, they should, God willing, make it safely through to Tuteville.

As they came out of the canyon, it seemed that God's will was not going to favour them. The canyon exit was blocked by Indians, Hunting Wolf at their head.

'What now, Dan?' Lillian Brennan asked shakily.

'That, Lillian,' Dan Mannion said, 'is one hell of a good question.'

Hunting Wolf came forward, pointing at Nathan Trump.

'You give Trump to Hunting Wolf. Hunting Wolf go.'

The outlaw, wild with panic, pleaded with Mannion, 'You can't just hand me over to that savage, Marshal. I'm your prisoner.'

Hunting Wolf said, 'Only Trump left. Give. Or Hunting Wolf kill all.'

'Marshal,' Trump whined. 'They'll roast me 'live.'

Dan Mannion snorted. 'I reckon your daddy did something awful to get this *hombre* so het up, Nathan. Looks like, with Zachariah in hell, this fella is going to take your pa's chicanery out of your hide.'

'Give Trump!' Hunting Wolf demanded.

A sudden and sad weariness gripped Mannion. 'I can't do that,' he told Hunting Wolf.

'Trump will face white man's justice.'

Hunting Wolf angrily rejected the marshal's stance. 'White man justice no good.' He pointed to Nathan Trump. 'Apache wronged. Apache justice.'

Mannion persisted, 'White man's justice. Trump hangs.'

Angrily, Hunting Wolf insisted, 'Apache justice!'

'I hope you understand, Lillian,' Dan Mannion said, 'that I just can't hand Nathan Trump over.'

Lillian Brennan smiled. 'I understand, Dan. Didn't think you would.'

The Tuteville marshal returned his gaze to Hunting Wolf. With finality, he said, 'White man's justice.'

Hunting Wolf looked to the darkening sky. He shouted an order, and the Indians dispersed into the rocks.

'When sun returns,' he promised, 'you all die!'

When Hunting Wolf rode away, Mannion said, 'We'd better find a niche in this canyon which will give us some chance.'

'Chance?' Trump snarled. 'There ain't no chance with 'Paches. They'll damn well butcher us all.' He sneered. ' 'Cept maybe you, Lil. They'll keep you for fun, I reckon.'

Raw fear stalked Lillian Brennan's eyes. Mannion's fist shot out to upend the outlaw. The marshal stood threateningly over the floored man and growled: 'You know, Trump. I'm already regretting not handing you over to Hunting Wolf. Push me again, and I will.'

Trump sullenly retreated, rubbing his swelling jaw and promising Mannion, 'Just one chance, Mannion. Just one damn chance.'

'Cuts both ways,' the marshal said grimly.

The night was long and edgy. The Indians kept up their constant chatter with the various animal calls by which they communicated when they were laying siege. Their exchanges were also designed to whittle away at their opponents' nerves. A sleepless, threat-filled night would wear their enemies down and make them less sharp once the sun blazed over the rim of the canyon and the battle began. Not that it would be much of a battle, with ammunition almost spent in the skirmish with Zachariah and Frank Trump. And there was no way that Mannion could put a gun in Nathan Trump's hand now, with the certainty of a hangman's noose in the offing. The outlaw had nothing to lose. A desperate man was a dangerous man.

Lillian Brennan came to sit alongside Dan Mannion. Briefly, he resented the intrusion on his thoughts of Rosie O'Sullivan, but he realized that Lillian had her fears and regrets, just as he had. His one big regret was that he had not made his love for Rosie known to her before he rode off on the fool's errand which now left him knocking on eternity's door.

'Are you hoping like me that it'll be quick, Dan?' Lillian asked.

'I guess,' he replied quietly.

Lillian Brennan was an intelligent woman, so he would not insult her by fobbing her off with false hope.

'Wife? she asked.

'No.'

'Woman?'

'Not sure.'

She smiled crookedly. 'Not sure?'

Mannion returned her smile. 'Didn't have the spit to tell Rosie how I felt about her before going after Nathan Trump.' He sighed wearily. 'I guess she'll never get to know now.'

Lillian said quietly, 'You could take your chance on making it out of here, Dan.'

The marshal settled curious eyes on her. 'Nathan and I are finished either way. Anyway, we deserve the predicament that we're in. You don't. So go.'

Dan Mannion took Lillian Brennan's hands in his, and told her sincerely, 'You're not facing a rope, Lillian.' Her eyes shone with hope. 'I'm not sending you back to Mexico.'

Wiping away tears, Lillian asked, 'When did you decide that?'

'Oh, before I wrangled with Zachariah and Frank Trump.'

She laughed softly. 'And I almost shot you, Marshal.'

'But you didn't, Lillian,' he said. 'And that's what counts.'

The new dawn was streaking the sky. Night would soon be over.

'Dan,' Lillian Brennan said.

'Ah-hah.'

'Mind if I kind of . . . nestle up?'

'Don't mind one little bit, Lillian,' Mannion said. 'In fact, I'd take it as a privilege.'

Cradled in the marshal's arms, Lillian said, 'Guess that girl of yours wouldn't like this canoodling any, Marshal.'

With world-weary sadness, Dan Mannion said, 'I reckon Rosie would understand, Lillian.'

After a spell, with the sky brightening rapidly, Mannion eased Lillian Brennan out of his arms and picked up his Winchester. Lillian's eyes held a world of troubled thought. She kissed Mannion on the cheek.

'You know, Dan,' she said. 'You're a whole lot like my late husband.'

Mannion said, 'Well, Lillian Brennan, if you picked him, I guess that's a mighty high compliment you just paid me.'

'Mighty high, indeed,' she confirmed.

The sun burst over the rim of the canyon. Lillian held her breath. Nathan Trump had retreated into himself; probably into madness. Mannion waited, his eyes keenly scanning the rocks for sign of the Apaches, but saw none. The stillness was absolute. The seconds dragged by into minutes, and the silence held. Ten. Fifteen. Twenty minutes. Still the silence held.

'You know, Lillian,' Dan Mannion said in disbelief, 'I think the Indians have vamoosed.'

'Are you sure, Dan?'

'I guess there's only one way to find out.'

The marshal stood up, offering himself as a perfect target. Lillian gasped. But a second later, when Dan was still standing, she was dancing with joy and hugging him. The reason for the Indians' departure became clear as they heard the sound of a bugle. Dan scrambled up to the rim of the canyon. Below on the desert plain the Apaches were on the run, with the cavalry in hot pursuit. Dan made his way back down from the rim to announce:

'Next stop, Tuteville!'

The marshal got a listless and gibbering Nathan Trump to his feet. The man was hardly worth hanging, he reckoned. Mannion felt a sudden breeze go past. An arrow thudded into the outlaw's throat. Mannion spun around, rifle hip high. Hunting Wolf was standing on top of a boulder high up in the canyon. He lowered his bow to his side. Mannion held his fire. Hunting Wolf stepped from the boulder and disappeared.

\*

The trail was tinged with the purples, greys, and orange of sunset when the gap leading to Tuteville was reached. Bone-weary, Mannion paused on the trail to look down on the town; his town. There were those who said that once the railroad arrived in a couple of years, Tuteville would become a city. Dan Mannion wasn't sure if he liked the idea. If that happened, old ways would change. Neighbours would become acquaintances instead of friends. Saloons, gambling-halls, brothels, and all the impedimenta of city life would arrive. The mayor had spoken of Dan becoming Tuteville City's Chief of Police. Is that what he'd want? More important, is that what Rosie Mannion would want? And if Rosie wasn't Rosie Mannion ... Well, nothing much would matter anyway.

Oblivious to the lurking threat posed by Wes Bellamy, Dan Mannion rode into the gap.

# TWENTY

Bellamy sprang off the shack's filthy bunk. His face, normally sharp of feature, was strained further by the wait for Dan Mannion's arrival. The marshal's approach had been the easy amble of a man whose job was done, and well done at that. With no need to pay attention to his surroundings, Mannion's and Lillian Brennan's ride through the gap was carefree. Their happy-go-lucky passage gave the bushwhacker timely warning of their approach.

Wes Bellamy hurried to the shack window. Wiping the grime from a patch of glass, he peered out. His smile was wolfish. His targets would be easy. He hadn't expected a woman to be riding with the marshal, but he had no qualms about dispatching her as well as him. He'd already taken the fee for her murder from Luther Barrett's pocket.

Before leaving the shack, Bellamy rolled and lit a smoke. He flicked the lucifer out of the window but unknown to him, the lit match struck the window frame and fell back on to the litter-strewn floor, where it fizzled.

'Almost home, Dan,' Lillian Brennan said. 'I bet that woman you've been thinking about will leap into your arms.'

Dan Mannion grinned. 'Hope so, Lillian.'

Lillian said, sincerely, 'She's a fool if she doesn't.'

The marshal's grin widened. 'If Rosie O'Sullivan doesn't say yes, maybe I'll call on you to point out the error of her ways, Lillian.'

'I have a feeling that she's just waiting to be asked, Dan.'

Mannion did not see Lillian Brennan's sad smile. His gaze had shifted to the smoke wafting through the window of the miner's shack high up in the gap, which was quickly followed by a shaft of orange flame bursting through the wall. Concerned that the shack might be occupied, Dan quickly changed direction to climb up the narrow track leading to the shack, just as a bullet twanged past him.

'Dismount!' he ordered Lillian.

Dan grabbed his rifle from its scabbard and flung himself from his horse. They huddled together, as two more rounds bit the ground inches from them. He shoved Lillian behind a nest of boulders. 'Stay there,' he ordered her. He grimly began his ascent through the rocks. 'This darn trail's got a whole bevy of vipers.'

Lillian watched breathlessly as Mannion ducked and weaved up through the gap, testing his luck to breaking point. Half-way up the track, he came to an abrupt halt on seeing Luther Barrett's battered and half devoured body. He could safely bet that the bushwhacker had been the rancher's killer. But why? And who was he?

As he got closer to the ambusher, the risk of being cut down became keener. But Mannion had no choice. He had to flush out the bushwhacker. He had gone through hell. Rosie O'Sullivan was waiting. And he'd not have his prize snatched from him now.

The ambusher had chosen well. Ahead of Mannion, directly in front of the bushwhacker's lair, cover was sparse, with a totally bare stretch which the marshal would have to leg it across to get to the killer. If he got to the cover directly below the assassin, it would mean that the shooter would have to take risks to nail him. That would even up the score. Mannion would then be confident of the outcome. He was of a mind that nothing was going to keep him from asking Rosie O'Sullivan to marry him.

As the marshal was readying himself for his last gamble of many, the gap filled with the thunder of hard-ridden horses. He glanced down into the gap to see a group of riders led by, to his utter dismay, Rosie O'Sullivan. He recognized Lew Cohen, Luther Barrett's foreman, and several Big B hands. Mannion's astonishment turned to horror as the ambusher opened up and dropped two of Luther Barrett's men. Rosie and the rest of the men scattered for cover.

Dan Mannion's next attention-getter was a clatter of stones and the scraping of boots from the ambusher's lair. He was making tracks.

'No, you don't!' the marshal growled, and launched himself in hot pursuit.

Rounding the boulder where Wes Bellamy had been, he spotted the assassin disappear into a stand of pine. Mannion knew that should he have to follow the man he now recognized as Bellamy into the trees, the risk to his health would be even greater than it had been up to now. He went on one knee, levelled his Winchester, steadied his aim, and fired. The Texan spun around, holding his shoulder. The Tuteville marshal wasted no time. He fired again. Bellamy teetered backwards, balancing for a second on the rim of the gap. Mercilessly, Mannion's rifle cracked a third time. The gunfighter was lifted off his feet and pitched down into the gap.

Relaxing on his haunches, Dan Mannion said, 'Let's hope that that's the last viper on this darn trail!'

On arriving down from the top of the gap, Rosie

O'Sullivan ran to Dan Mannion's arms and covered his face with kisses

'Oh, Dan, thank God you came back safe to me.'

On the way back to Tuteville, Rosie explained the sequence of events which had led to Luther Barrett's death, and Wes Bellamy's attempt to kill Mannion.

'A ranch hand from the Rusty Spur, the Big B's neighbour, spotted Luther headed towards the gap while he was out searching for strays. When he heard of Luther's disappearance, he recalled seeing him.'

Mannion said, 'Remind me to invite that ranch hand to our wedding, Rosie.'

'Wedding?'

'Well,' the Tuteville marshal chuckled, 'a woman can't kiss a man like you just did,' Rosie O'Sullivan blushed redder than an English rose, 'and not accept his proposal of marriage, I reckon.'

When her heart settled down to some semblance of ordered rhythm, Rosie said, 'I reckon you're right at that, Marshal Mannion.'

It was eight months later. Mr and Mrs Mannion were saying goodbye to Lillian Brennan.

'I'm going to miss your help round the bath-house, Lillian,' Rosie said. 'But more important, I'm going to miss your friendship.'

Lillian said, 'Someday, who knows, I might get

back to Tuteville for a visit. Or you lovebirds might make it to Utah.'

'Best be getting along, Lillian,' the tall, large-eyed man called from the waiting wagon.

'Coming, John,' Lillian called back.

Saddened, Dan and Rosie Mannion watched the wagon roll out of town. Lillian Brennan's leaving would leave a gap in their lives, but they had fond memories and a coming event to fill the void.

'You know, Dan,' Rosie said, 'If this kicking mule inside me turns out to be a female, I'd like to name her Lillian.'

The man called John Lacey had come to town looking for a wife to replace the one he had buried on the plains three weeks previously. Maybe one day he'd fall in love with Lillian Brennan, and she with him. But right now all that they both needed was a fresh start.

Lillian Brennan did not look back as she left, fearful that her love for Dan Mannion, which she had successfuly hidden for eight torturous months, would shine forth like a beacon. There were some who would say that she was lucky, and maybe she was. John Lacey seemed to be a good man. Only time would tell.

But the luckiest woman alive was Rosie Mannion.